IN DREAMS
OF DRAGONS

—•—

SONYA LAWSON

SAUCEBOX PRESS

Contents

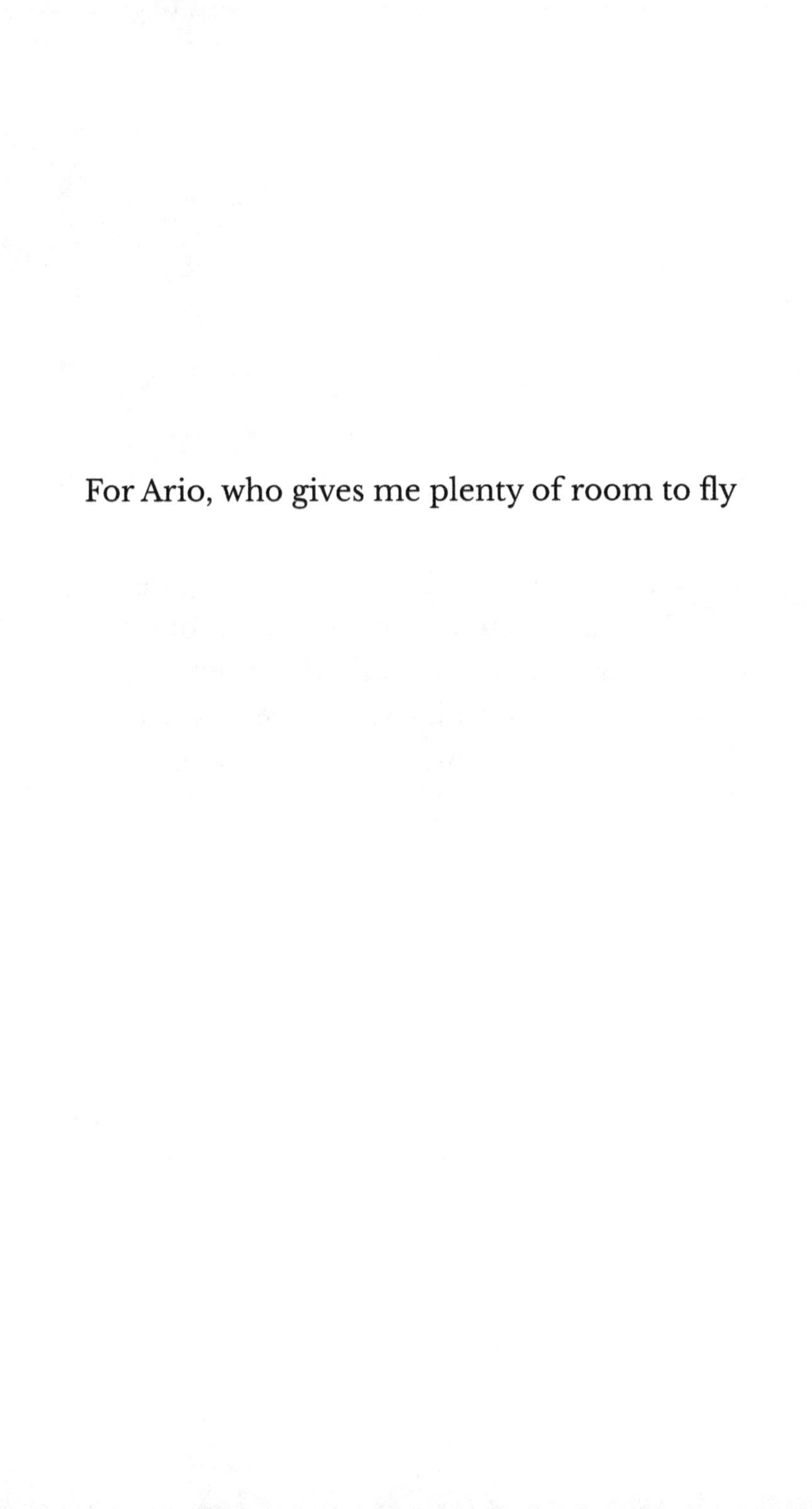

For Ario, who gives me plenty of room to fly

ONE

A ROAR WENT UP in the Great Hall when my husband held the severed head high for all to see. As Lord Ingar, he commanded the attention of the room, but the massive feast commemorating the hunt and the bloody evidence of his success ensured every guest in the Great Hall remained mesmerized by their lord.

From my position behind my towering husband, I could only see the back of the head. It was enough in the moment, what with viscera still trailing and blood splattered across its shimmery hide.

"No more shall beasts such as this terrorize our land, hoard its resources, keep us from what is ours by right and might," Blaine howled to the crowd. I couldn't see his face, but I saw his body shake with the force of his words, the head in his grip swaying with each thrust of his arm. The hair he gripped was full, dark as tar, and looked silken to the touch despite being drenched in blood and filled with debris. Its skin was a kaleidoscope of colors in the dull torchlight—milky white and pale one moment, dark and dusky the next, olive-toned then sandy, giving way to fantastical greens and blues and purples. It was like every color of every being I'd ever seen in my lifetime dipped in an opalescent sheen.

Lord Ingar looked over his shoulder at me and gave a wink, flirtatious and indulgent at once. "My new wife, the lovely Lady Roselle of Ingar," he boomed, looking from me back at the crowd, "has yet to have the pleasure of witnessing our mastery over this creature, our dominance in this land. Until tonight!"

Another roar and round of claps and table-pounding made my ears ring. Blaine turned fully toward me then, and I peeked at him with a soft smile—partially to be demure, as was expected, and partially to not glimpse the face of the thing still gripped tightly in his fist. "For you, my lady, my wife. The first successful dragon hunt this year. We present the spoils in your honor."

I looked at Blaine fully then and nodded. I was lucky this was all any expected me to do in the moment, because once I saw it fully, the face, I instantly became entranced by the dead, lavender eyes staring straight into my own. With a thud and a cheer, my husband threw the head down in my line of sight, an offering as promised, a prize for his bride of one season.

I knew little of dragons beyond my studies of the tales as a pupil, part of the training all ladies received when they reached maturity. The stories told of dragons' treachery and magic, their disregard for life, their strain on the lands of men. They were the scourge, the enemy, the very real monster lurking outside our castle gates—according to my guardians and tutors, and now, my husband. Here was one staring straight at me, its unblinking lavender eyes wide and serpentine. The tongue, a pale pink the color of a fresh piglet, flopped out, forked and long, a tool to lick and lash and expel their destructive flames. Scorch marks trailed across the muzzle, remnants of a fire now banked. Sharp teeth hid behind lips frozen in a yell or scream, a look of disdain and aggression fossilized in the moment of death. Again, those lavender eyes, very much dead, seemed to see still, know, judge, and find lacking. Blood trickled down the strings of meat trailing the throat of the dragon, yet all I could focus on were those eyes, clear and angry yet somehow assured. It was a complex look for a simple, destructive creature. I studied it, as I did all things

I found visually fascinating, thinking about how I could capture the creature in a tapestry, weave the look with thread and time, if possible.

"Lady," Blaine said on a roaring laugh, turning to acknowledge me after long minutes lost in his tale of heroics, while I was lost in that haunting look. "I do hope you like your gift. It cost much in time and blood."

"Oh, my lord. Were you injured?" I gasped, a small fear pushing through my mind at the thought.

He laughed again. "I see my wife was not paying heed to my tale of action and bravery. No matter. We shall have time tonight to have words, and much more."

A hoot went up as a blush flashed across my cheeks. I was new to this, the intimacy between a man and woman, even if I knew much about it before my time. Living in a castle, even as a lady, often meant seeing and hearing a great deal before the wedding night. Still, I had been taught to be polite, civil, and chaste in all things, to not discuss what I saw or knew, to think only of duty and bloodlines.

Lord Ingar vaulted across the table, causing the dragon's head to skid to the side and topple to the floor. I wanted to catch it, lay it gently, and give it proper observance and respect, even if it was a monster. I knew my husband would mount it; there were similar kills lining the high ceilings of the Great Hall where we feasted. I had been avoiding looking at them as best I could. They disturbed me in ways I wished not to think on. However, this head would draw my attention wherever it was stuffed and hung, and I would not be able to help search for the lavender eyes that had been so close to my own for a few moments. Not yet mounted, it snared my focus, drew my attention from the floor where it was discarded and forced me to think on the horrors this creature visited on the surrounding lands, what it could have done with its life if it lived. Even, with a pang of realization, what it must have suffered in death.

I jolted out of my dark, twisting thoughts when I felt a hard tug and landed in the arms of my husband, who laughed and carried me off as jeers and chuckles echoed in our wake.

Blaine deposited me on the bed. He was not harsh, nor was he gentle. I was a load released with ease.

"I tell you, Roselle, I shall hunt these beasts far more often. I forget the feeling between battles. Now it rages in me. My father went out several times each season. I must do the same, to protect my people. To protect you, my Little Light." He bent down, and his dark beard scratched my face in a lovely way as he gently kissed my lips. When he pulled back, his deep-brown eyes swirled with a heat I had come to recognize and anticipate.

Still, I had questions. "You hunt as needed, yes?" I asked. The dragon hunt commenced through necessity, not pleasure. Surely?

He chuckled, ignoring the question for a time. Instead of offering answers, he began undressing as he walked to the water jug in the corner of the room, to strip and splash water on his face. He was now naked from the chest up, his muscles bunching and pulling as he rinsed wine and food and other things from his beard. Blaine was a strong, solid man with height and muscle and the authority to use both in many ways, be that hunting as he wished or bedding his wife. I was new to this life of wife and lady to a lord, but there were times when the fire of the sconces on the walls caught the rivulets of water running down Blaine's firm chest and stomach in such a way heat fluttered in my belly.

He swiped cloth against his wet face and chest, a smirk in my direction when he finally replied. "Dragons are to be hunted at all times, whenever possible."

"What of their destruction, the chaos they cause? Is there a season when they are more active?" I wanted answers, something to help me push those lavender eyes out of my mind, dismiss the confused mix of emotions I felt when they stared at me from the bloody head on the banquet table. The look of them, the pain and confusion and awareness, was not what I had always pictured in my mind when considering the things—these supposedly mindless destroyers who ruined our world for long ages before they were hunted near to extinction. If they were mindless beasts, encroaching on the lands of men to feed on people and destroy our world, I could shove away the feelings I discovered that evening, push them to the side in service of the greater good.

"You know our history as well as I."

"I know tales of old, yes. Yet I have heard no recent stories."

"Because we hunt," Blaine stated with surprising vehemence. My husband was a jovial, kind man who enjoyed drink and food and laughter, but in this subject, he was unyielding. "Our world is safe because we hunt the creatures before they do us harm."

"Oh" was all I could get out before my husband reached me, taking my head firmly in his own and bending down to give me a hungry kiss. He tasted of ale and other more vital things. I told myself the hint of coppery blood was in my imagination, all to do with the events of the evening and the odd feelings and ideas running around in my mind.

He deepened the kiss, bending me farther until my back reached the bed and his weight made me sink down. Blaine pulled up only to start unlacing the front of my evening dress, tugging hard on the ribbons threaded there until it loosened to his liking. He dove his hand in, touching my heated flesh, and I whimpered softly at the scrape of his rough hands against me.

"Up," Blaine commanded, pulling himself free of my dress to grab my arms and right me to sitting. I was dazed, by kisses and events and odd ideas running through my mind. He shoved the bodice of my dress wide enough to rip it up and over my head, leaving only my thin, lightly dyed chemise. Reaching around, a grin on his face as it came level to my own, he loosened my skirts and swiftly lifted my thighs so he could slip the mounds of material down my legs.

More heat filled his brown gaze as he pushed me back to lie on the bed, staring at the juncture of my thighs not quite visible because of the thin whisper of fabric between us. His hands clenched my hips and said, "Do you wish to hear of the hunt?" The idea excited him, I could tell. His breath rushed out in soft pants. The excitement was contagious, as I felt my own heat and hunger rising to meet his.

I only nodded, sparks of want running across my skin and a desire to know racing through my mind.

He lay beside me on the bed, skimming his hands low to reach under my chemise, and his tongue licked my ear as he whispered dark things. "A neighboring lord sent word of a dragon encroaching our lands, hiding along the northern ridge. I found it easily. When I arrived, only a few soldiers at my back, I bid them wait away from the cave unless I called for reinforcements. I wished to engage the thing alone."

His fingers were doing delicious things to my core, stroking and circling in the growing wetness there, as he continued.

"It was formidable, dripping with magics and heat. Much like you, my delicious wife. It writhed and fought, but even its scorching flames were no match for my steel."

The moment the heat inside me built almost to bursting, his hands disappeared, leaving me wanting and aching in a way I could never verbalize to him. Blaine rose above me, pushing the fabric up so he could enter me while still talking in rough whisper. "Its head came off easily, staining my blade and the floor of the wretched cave. I strode out a true ruler, protecting his people from the scourge of such a beast."

My body jerked from the force of his movements, and I felt heat grow and swell again, but as often occurred, his pace increased too quickly, became too jerky, and he finished. After a few moments of rest to collect his breath, Blaine rolled to the side and rubbed a hand over my belly. "Tonight, I plant my child in you, just as I slew that dragon. I know it. It will grow to be a strong son who will slay many himself."

My breath hitched at his vision, not of a dragon-slayer but of a baby boy who was part of me, someone I could know and understand and love completely. I covered Blaine's hand with my own and squeezed. He looked on me with a silly grin, one he rarely gave outside these bedroom walls, and my heart stuttered. Blaine was a good man, a good husband. He would be a good father someday.

I cleaned myself at the water jug as Blaine threw back the furs and climbed underneath. He patted his chest, a silent command to lie across him. Hugging me tight, he hummed in contentment and said, "It has been a grand day, Little Light."

I nodded in agreement. It was grand. Even if the lavender eyes of the dragon were still fresh in my mind as I chased sleep.

Even if this day marked the beginning of the end of all I knew.

Two

My mother sat alone with me every night of my life with her, from the time I was a babe, I assume, up to the accident that killed both her and my father when I was nine years old. Every night, my mother dismissed any maids or nurses in attendance, tucked me firmly in bed, then sat beside me. Sometimes she sang. Sometimes she told me old tales. Sometimes she talked of current events and future plans, seeking my reaction and gently guiding me in her own way. Regardless of what she did in the night, she ended each one the same. A soft kiss on my forehead, a pat on my stomach, and a whispered phrase: "In dreams there is knowing, so find sweet knowledge this night, my love."

On certain dream-filled nights, I would remember her sweet words. Occasionally I would dream vividly. When I was with my mother, we would discuss dreams at breakfast in an offhanded way, speculating on meaning, though she had always advised me to heed my dreams. I never knew if she had similar dreams. She never confessed such things to me. However, I suspect as much. She knew too much of dreaming to not experience the same shock of images and events I did from an early age.

I did not hide my dreams so much as simply stopped discussing them. Upon the deaths of my parents, I was shuttled off my homelands to stay with guardians and tutors, and I had no one to speak with about them. My guardians betrothed me to Blaine rather quickly. All were shocked I was not already betrothed, as many highborn ladies were at birth. I was considered old for such a task, so my distant cousin, who was a considerate if distant overseer of my life, accepted the betrothal offer on the condition I was allowed to wait until age twenty-two, far later than usual. The previous Lord Ingar grumbled but took the concession, and I saw Blaine occasionally for over a decade before our wedding. However, I did not speak with him alone often, did not talk with him about internal matters or thoughts. I did what tutors and guardians and chaperones advised, growing to find a comfort in my future husband, if not an undying love or full companionship. I thought it would come with time, after marriage, and there would be mornings in my future when I could once again discuss my dreams with someone I loved and who loved me.

Even if that time came, we had not been there on the night of the feast for the hunt, on the night I began dreaming of those lavender eyes. Sometimes I stuttered to life in my dreams, coming to realization slowly. Not so that night. I felt shoved into my dream, as if I had stumbled hard into the hot gray haze often present in my dreamscapes. It shifted and curled around me, thickening until it practically blinded. It parted to show my mother standing on a mountainside in the distance, lingering outside a small cave entrance. It was the range around Ingar, one I saw daily now but had never fully explored. She stood tall, as she had in life, assurance in her stance and her look. Her gown, a lavender gossamer, fluttered in the breeze like thin, delicate wings, wrapping up and around her as she stood unmoving, a direct contrast to the fabric all around her. Her blonde hair, the same nearly white shade as mine, was tight to her head, falling in a long braid over her shoulder. Her icy-blue eyes held the attention of my own, their mirror, as her look turned from concern to sadness to a soft smile. She waved at me, in good-bye or as a beckoning I could not decipher, and heaved a sigh. After looking back into the cave for a moment, she whipped her head around quickly and narrowed her stare in my direction, her face morphing into a sharp-toothed, menacing grimace, pink forked tongue flicking out in a rapid beat to lick her curled lips.

The haze came again, hot and engulfing, swirling me until I found myself in the halls of Ingar Keep, running at full speed, a lump of fear lodged firmly in my throat. Behind me was a dark shape, an unknowable blob of form, the only distinguishing feature the glowing lavender eyes focused on me. I rounded a familiar corner to see the door of our bedchamber up ahead. I slammed through it, not bothering to open and close it. Natural order may not exist in my dream state, but fear pounded regardless.

The room was all fire and black smoke, the smell hot and fierce, the crackle near deafening. Blaine stood in the center of the room naked and bloodied. I could not tell if the blood covering his body was his own or from another. He turned, fierce and wild, with a bloodied broadsword clutched in his hands. His fierce face found mine, and he stopped, looking lost and confused at what he saw, shaking his head in disbelief. I tried to reach for him, call out to him, but the smoke and fire kept us separated and unable to hear anything over the roar it created. In seconds, my husband's face twisted from confusion and hurt to anger. He glared in my direction, gripped his sword tighter, and wrenched his mouth in what could either be a scream or a cry—I could not decipher—as the flames swallowed the sound. The blaze engulfed him, swallowing up my husband from my sight, forcing me to turn away.

Those lavender eyes appeared again in the shadows of the destructive glow, and I turned to run from both—the eyes and the flames. I ran, unknowing, through the keep, the heat at my back pushing me forward, until I wound my way up a flight of stairs I'd never seen to a tower room I did not know, where a small, dingy straw bed lay surrounded by singe marks. This place brought fear with it as well, though I did not understand why or how. I was trapped then, between fire and that room that sent a hard blast of ice through my veins, not knowing where to go next, which fear to confront or charge. A scream turned to an animal roar, then turned to the roar of an inferno. I ducked, cowered under my own arms in a ball on the floor of that room that felt so horrible for some unknown reason, and let my own scream rip through my throat.

The cry that escaped my lips in real life, as I lay next to my husband, was no scream. More a whimper. Yet it was enough to pull me from the awful place I inhabited in my sleep. I blinked in the darkness and shuddered out a breath, as the adrenaline of fear raged in my veins still, until I was calm enough to bring a shaking hand to my brow, wipe away the sweat, and let out a shuddered, harsh breath, a mix of relief and confusion.

THREE

After such dreamings, my stomach was a churning, nervous mess at breakfast the next day. Blaine was once again telling the tale of the dragon hunt to any who would listen. Luckily, the dragon head was no longer on the table. Someone had likely spirited it away to be mounted. A shudder went down my spine at the thought of those lavender eyes staring at me from up high in the coming days. On that thought, I tuned in briefly to the harrowing tale of bravery my husband recounted and felt someone watching me. This was nothing new. As Lady of Ingar Keep, many minded my behavior to immolate or judge. Even before, when I was the daughter of another lord in another castle, someone always watched and assessed. Here, however, a certain hard glare fell on me often. Master Codiff, my husband's top adviser and a mage, stared with a quizzical look creasing his brow. He moved his gaze from my husband to me and back again, noting my immersion, noting all he could about me and what I did. He looked almost as if he could read my thoughts, see the outline of my dream, feel my shudder himself. Four months of intense scrutiny from this man, ever since Blaine brought me to his castle after our marriage, yet I remained unnerved by his look and presence. I knew little rest or privacy indeed—or possibly even thought—whenever Master Codiff's cold stare turned my way.

My blue eyes clashed with his nearly black ones, but I skittered mine away, a revulsion I tramped down daily threatening to claw its way up my throat. Even more than the lavender eyes from last evening, or any dragon who still had their head, I feared Codiff. He had my husband's ear, unfailingly, in a way I did not yet have. Maybe never would. He stalked the halls of the keep, pristine white-and-gold robes billowing in his wake, his silver hair and beard trailing. His stare was always hard as coal, holding more judgment and disdain than I had ever felt in my previous twenty-two years of life. Sometimes, when he knew his study would not be interrupted by the only person he felt mattered—Lord Ingar—his stare was blatant and sharp, his chin tucked neatly against his long steepled fingers and his head cocked in a mix of morbid curiosity and ill regard. I had done no harm to the man that I knew, so there was no logical reason I could deduce for such waves of distrust from him, but it was there nonetheless, marring every day in Ingar.

This morning, however, he felt the need to add sharp words to his stare. "My lady," he said with a dip of his already-deep voice and an inflection that made me feel like a wayward child about to be disciplined. "I see you eat little. Are you not well?"

Anyone listening may believe the mage showed concern. He did not. He wished to call out my behavior in some way, point to some action as an issue deserving of scrutiny and possible reprimand. He did not intend to elicit a response from me, but from my husband, who, at the question, turned from his hunting tale to look me up and down.

"Lady Roselle, you must eat more," Blaine called, leaning over to inch my plate piled with bread and cheese and dried meats closer to the edge of the table. "If you wish to grow me a son, you need take care of your body."

I nodded, giving him a tight smile as I picked up a hunk of cheese and began to eat. My stomach was not ready for food this early. It roiled, rebelling against the idea as I swallowed it down. My husband looked on with concern, while Master Codiff stared with grim pleasure at my discomfort.

Deciding to take focus off my plate, my mouth, and what my body did or did not do, I began to question my husband. "What of your plans this day, Lord?"

He laughed, hearty and full, before tearing off a chunk of dried boar and chewing through his reply. "I must train my men, attend business, meet with my people who need assistance. It is a usual day for a lord, my lady. And what of you? How does your tapestry fare?"

I beamed at his question, forgetting dragons and mages for a moment. I'd finished two small tapestries for Ingar Keep prior, idyllic scenes that hung in back corridors. I had a much grander project, a rendition of Ingar lands with Blaine. I worked diligently to bring my design to life, to weave with skill and focus to create a perfect image in thread. I hoped to hang it in the mostly barren Great Hall, a tribute to my new home made by my hand for all to see.

"It fares well, thank you. It is a large piece, requiring much detail work, but it is close to completion. Another week or so and it will be done."

"A fine display, I am sure. A testament to your domestic talents and concerns," Blaine answered in praise.

"Quite," Codiff said, the hint of a sneer in his voice something only I seemed to hear. He paused momentarily, appearing to ponder some issue or idea, then continued in a more thoughtful tone. "On the topic of domestic duties, my lady, it may be best you spend some time today in the markets. The people have seen little of you of late, aside from those who frequent the Great Hall of course."

"Is this so?" my husband asked. "When was the last time you visited the markets, wife?"

I shrunk a little in on myself. The markets were a bustling place, full of people and products of all varieties. As a child, I had loved market days, but as I grew older, I enjoyed such outings less and less, preferring to stay in the spaces I knew with familiar people close at hand. I also felt ill at ease in large crowds, always had. Market days, with the hustling pace of commerce and the ever-changing landscape of stalls and people, felt stifling, caging in some way.

Every part of Ingar was new to me, as were the people. In the keep I had a small amount of control in where I went and whom I interacted with during my days. Not complete control, but some. I also knew what to expect in the spaces I frequented. It was not so in the Ingar market, which was even larger than the markets I had occasionally visited before coming here. The layout was a winding maze of people, animals, and stalls where one could lose their way if not careful.

Eventually, I answered softly, "About a month, husband."

"Oh, that will not do," he said, a shake of his head. "I expect you to act as lady in all ways, for all people, Roselle. This is a disappointment."

Rising from his seat, scooting my own out as he pulled away from the table, he commanded, "Come. Come. You are now to go to market before fulfilling any of your other duties today. Codiff, assign a guard and ensure my lady stays safe as she does as I bid."

I looked back at the mage, saw a malevolent grin on his face, and knew market day would not be enjoyable for me for a variety of reasons.

FOUR

MY MARKET OUTING WOULD occur after the noon meal. Having had more than enough of Master Codiff's stares while I attempted to eat, I decided to forego the Great Hall. It was not demanded of me, as the afternoon meal was far more casual in most keeps with the continual comings and goings of its inhabitants through the daytime hours. I often ate light noon meals at my tapestry, in my receiving room, or, my personal favorite, in a small corner of the keep kitchens.

Kitchens were a comforting place for me. Not only because they were warm and snug, but the buzz of directed and synchronized activity soothed something in me. I appreciated the skill of cooking as well as the outcome of the efforts, but the process itself was fascinating. I was not allowed to cook myself; a lady was above such things, according to my guardians and tutors. Though I do remember my mother occasionally entering the kitchen not to observe but to participate. Stew was a particular specialty for her, one she had lovingly created for her family often enough that so many years later, I could taste the herb-crusted meats and spiced root vegetables on my tongue.

Ingar Keep's kitchen was a cavernous place, with a bevy of nooks and crannies from where I could sit and observe. I did this for a time, and the people of the kitchens gave me a wide berth, perhaps fearing I were there to evaluate or judge. Not so. I wished only to be an observer of the process, feel the controlled rush of the kitchen, even if I could not step in myself. In my first week at Ingar Keep, when I felt most lost and out of place in my new home, I stole off to the kitchen daily and commandeered a small stool in a shadowed corner, a spot where I could look on and feel the familiarity of activity, even if the place was different. That changed, however, when Palle warmed to me.

Palle was the head cook, the ruler of the kitchens of Ingar. She worked her underlings with a firm but guiding hand, something I witnessed for days before she turned that same critical concern my way. I had of course formally been introduced to her on my first day. Lady Ingar was expected to command the direction of the kitchen though was not allowed to participate in the running of it in any tangible way. Therefore, Palle was one of the first head of service I met on my arrival, directly after the head housekeeper and prior to the master gardener. I took little interest in the others beyond the practical. There was not much I enjoyed in cleaning or gardening, although I appreciated the skill and work it took to achieve both. Cooking, however, fascinated me, so I looked on the head cook with more care.

Palle was an aged woman, though by no means ancient. If forced to guess, by the lines on her face and the streaks of kinky gray hair standing out against the deep brown dominating her head, I would say she was in her sixth decade of life. She was an age that brought with it honed skill and an ability to work her body effectively in service of such skill. She was round in shape, sturdy and agile in her kitchen domain. I only ever saw her in the kitchen uniform she wore: brown linen shirt with the sleeves rolled up over strong forearms, brown skirt falling to her ankles, strong leather boots blacked with grease and soot from the hearths, and a thick apron, a blue so deep and dark it hid the stains of time and use well, showing only the occasional flash of flour or dribble of light liquid. Her ever-present cloth, uncolored cotton hanging in a strip from a loop she must have sewn onto her apron for such a purpose, was ready to wipe up stray bits and splashes when needed to keep both her person and her workspace clean.

And the kitchens of Ingar Keep stayed surprisingly clean. Kitchen maids were required to sweep and wipe and straighten as they worked, a standing order from their head cook. I'd never seen the like—mess was always a part of the kitchen in my experience—but the contained chaos of Ingar's kitchen made for a smooth workday. People cleaned as they cooked, working behind others efficiently because of this, and everything returned to its assigned place by day's end, so that her staff never wasted precious time in search of tools or ingredients. It was a glimpse of genius, a study at what one, who knew what they were about and were not afraid to make changes or enforce rules, could do when they had free rein.

Because this space was so well run, my presence the first week had not gone unnoticed. I, however, being new to my home, had no idea sitting quietly in a dark corner had had much effect. Palle startled me on the fifth day when she barked out, "Lady Ingar." It was a command to halt if I ever heard one, which was startling enough from a servant. I'd heard her give similar commands to her workers and had frozen in place, shocked by her address to me and, oddly, wondering what I could have possibly done wrong to snag her attention.

She had finished placing a row of spliced chickens on a spit to turn in the large hearth, wiped her hands on the cloth at her waist, and squinted at me. "Is there a particular reason you come to the kitchens daily?"

"Yes" was all I had said in answer, not wishing to give too much away in this new place, to this cook I barely knew.

She pulled straight, crossed her arms at her ample chest, and huffed out in defiance. "If you have issue with my kitchen or the food, I would appreciate an up-front answer and discussion."

I blinked, taken aback by her honesty and forthright nature. I was new to being Lady Ingar but had been raised a lady nonetheless. Servants, even head servants, did not often speak in such ways to ladies. I wasn't offended. Instead, she pulled me into her commanding orbit even more.

Offering quick reassurance, I gave her more information. "Oh no, Palle. You run your kitchen with excessive efficiency. Your food is beyond reproach. I have no notes or directions for you. I just... I like kitchens. The warmth, the smell, the bustle. I find them soothing spaces. As Ingar Keep is still so new to me..."

Palle had nodded then, clasping her hands together with a definitive crack that I knew meant I did not need to say more. "All is well, my lady. I feared you had issue, but I see you do not. However, if you do, at any time, let me know and we shall discuss your concerns like civilized, intelligent women. Yes?"

I nodded, smiled, and she gave me a tight grin back, the only type of smile I ever saw her give, before she asked a maid to move my stool to the large workbench in the center of the kitchen. "If you are to spend time with us, Lady Ingar, you should not do so in the shadows."

I had taken my new seat, a seat I occupied often from then on, and chatted amiably with Palle as she worked.

It became an almost daily occurrence, even after I became more accustomed to the keep and my husband and had more responsibilities and duties tugging at my time and attention. I came to the kitchen for spells several times a week, soothed by the warmth, the smells, the tastes, and the gruff but kind chatter of Palle. I knew little of my assigned ladies-in-waiting, talked to them only in polite ways about small subjects of little importance. With Palle, however, every conversation was about learning or easing, advising or comforting, and I had grown to appreciate her strong, consistent presence in my life.

On that market day, I wandered to the kitchen an hour before the noon meal. Palle and her workers were scurrying, preparing foods for the table. Noon meal was more casual, with platters of food set out neatly on sideboards for people to graze as they needed for a few hours in the afternoon. As maids piled chilled meats, hunks of cheese, fruit, and bread on large oval dishes, Palle directed others in the cooking of the evening meal. Kitchen maids peeled and sliced small hills of potatoes and carrots while Palle trimmed the last in a line of huge sides of beef for roasting.

"Lady Ingar," she called, barely looking up from the beef she sliced with precision and speed. "How are you this fine morning?"

"All is well, though I am hungry."

Palle waved her large butcher's knife in a way I would call haphazard if it were any other person, and said, "Help yourself."

I grinned at her ease with me, her familiarity, the way she commanded the kitchen as hers even if I was Lady Ingar of Ingar Keep. The kitchen was hers, even if it took up space in my keep, and I knew this. I enjoyed it even.

I grabbed a wooden plank and piled various bits and pieces on top, planning to eat enough

here to make up for a mostly misspent breakfast and the lunch I would skip. After pulling
myself onto my stool and thanking the maid
who offhandedly offered me a tin cup of water,
I ate in earnest. My ease in the space, as well
as the sight and smell of all the fresh food,
awakened my stomach.

Palle worked and I ate in silence, happy to be
warm and in an active space where I was not the
center of attention. As she finished trimming
the meat, Palle looked up and asked, "Do you
have plans for a long excursion this afternoon?"
with her brow raised at my pile of food. She
gave her usual grin after, a sign she teased without bite, and I nodded.

I swallowed a bite. "I'm to go to market today.
I've apparently been remiss in my duties as
Lady Ingar." There was a joke in my tone, but
also an edge of bitterness at the way events had
played out earlier in the day.

"Bah. You've done none such. Market days are
all well and good, but you run this keep just
fine."

"Thank you," I replied, looking down at the
food to not show how much her offhanded
assessment rallied me. "There are reasons I
should attend market more often, mix with the
people outside the keep on a regular basis."

"True," Palle said, assessing me, "but you do well here. You are still new to Ingar and our ways. Do not expect yourself to be everything to the people all at once. Mainly because the people, us folk not in your noble ranks, have other things to do than worry about you lot all the time."

I chuckled at the truth and practicality of her jest and finished my meal as Palle talked of her day, what she had done, and her plans for the evening meal. When I cleared my plate, I took it to the washing bin, unwilling to leave it lying in the kitchen where everyone cleaned up after themselves. Palle had tried to stop me from doing this before but to no avail, so she generally ignored it.

"I am off to prepare for market," I called, heading toward the door. "Anything in particular you may need or want, Palle?"

"No, my lady. We are fine here. However, feel free to send along anything you see and want. We'll accommodate."

"Until next time," I called.

"Tomorrow or, at most, the day after," Palle said in response, then snorted at her own joke regarding my predictability.

"Yes. Yes. More than likely tomorrow." I grinned as I left, buoyed in spirit by my visit to the kitchens, feeling full and warm, both from the food and the time spent in Palle's company.

FIVE

THE MARKET SMELLED LIKE people, animals, food, and manure all mixed together in a dish left to sit overnight. The din was chaotic, with yells and banter and whispers combining with the brays of animals and the stomping of feet and the chopping of wood and other meaty things, making it near impossible to identify a single noise or conversation. The sights of rushed bodies, swaying mammals, glittering coins, and colorful fruit had my eyes darting around constantly. It was truly too much for the senses. I usually spent quiet days attending small duties as a young lady, then as Lady Ingar. Blaine was correct to admonish me for ignoring my other concerns, such as mingling with the people on market days, but the chaos of the square was almost too much to take.

I eventually eased into it. The caged feeling lingered, gnawing at the back of my mind, though it lessened with time as I hung back with a cadre of guards and whispering ladies-in-waiting who swooped in to straighten my skirts or hold a basket I might fill with goods. I knew Codiff lurked somewhere, likely in the shadows. I felt his stare watching for any misstep during my outing.

Soon enough, I saw things that fascinated my artistic inclinations, things I could add to my work in the future. The bulk of the guard, realizing I was not venturing too far afield, began to wander farther away, and the ladies-in-waiting, all women connected far more to Lord Blaine than myself after these few short months, stayed well behind me, choosing to not interact in any way. I was fine with it, as it meant I did not need to explain to anyone my desire to stare at the way the smithy's sparks flew out in an arch of wild oranges and yellows and shifted to black-and-gray ash when they hit the cobblestone street. Or how the gleam of bright-red apples contrasted beautifully with the softly buzzing cloud of fruit flies hovering inches above.

Minutes staring led to tentative conversations with a few merchants and the purchasing of a few wares and goods. Everyone was kind enough, if a little aloof. All seemed as unsure as I was, all in attendance trying out the fairly novel practice of speaking as or to Lady Roselle of Ingar Keep.

I was wandering aimlessly with two guards along the stalls when I spotted the remainder of the group sent by my husband to protect me. Four burly men who often attended me in and outside of the castle huddled around something, hungry looks on their faces. I stopped cold when I saw why they circled so. A small girl—no more than fourteen at most—carrying a basket filled to the brim with eggs, was being shoved to and fro among them. They grabbed at her as, pulling on her hair and skirts as they shoved her from man to man. They said things in deep, rumbling tones, things I was too far away to hear but was woman enough to imagine from the look of stark fear and horror on the child's face.

I had been timid in this place, new and uncertain and therefore soft in step and deed. Yet I had not always been so, and a sudden, surprising flash of lavender eyes in my mind made my spine snap straight and my steps fall sure and steady as I glided to the quartet harassing the girl.

They were young men, but strapping nonetheless, and towered over the poor child, who I could now see was shaking because of what had been said and done to her. I was within steps, still unnoticed, when one of the two men at my back gave a sharp whistle. The four focused solely on their prey, unaware I observed on their actions until I was directly beside them. They pulled up to attention, but in such a way that they trapped the girl within their ranks.

"What is the meaning of this?"

"My lady?" one of the guards countered, clearly confused.

"Why do you treat this child so?" I asked, giving my most haughty and disapproving sniff.

"Who? Milly? Why, Milly's no little child," another answered in a condescending tone.

Heat rose in my words and my face. "You correct your lady in public?"

"Lady Ingar, no, I meant—"

Pulling a hand up, I said, "I care not what you meant. Leave her be. Allow her to pass this instant."

The guards looked mutinous but obeyed direct orders, giving the girl named Milly the tiniest of spaces to pass between them. She darted out and skidded to a stop before me, dropping to a deep curtsey.

"Lady Ingar, I thank you for your kind consideration. 'Specially for one such as me."

"Rise, girl, please." When she did but continued to look away from me, I stepped closer. "Milly, is it?"

She nodded and I continued in a quiet voice.

"I would like you to look on me, Milly."

When the girl did, my breath stopped. Golden-orange eyes the color of amber and nearly as shining peeked at me quickly before looking down at the ground. "Oh, I cannot, my lady. Do forgive me."

"I only wish to see for myself you are well," I said in a soft tone, mesmerized by another set of eyes, filing them away along with the lavender dragon stare. The color was arresting, to be sure, but the glimpse of emotion in those lovely eyes, the pain and uncertainty and relief, shocked my system.

"Aye, my Lady Ingar." She curtsied again. "All is well." Quietly she said, "Nothing I am not used to."

That brought me back to myself, to the reasons for this encounter, and I considered the guards behind Milly. They looked off behind me, seeming not to care, as I attempted to help Milly.

"May I escort you somewhere, dear girl? Are you off to sell your eggs to market? I could accompany you, if you would like."

"Oh, no my lady. I could not ask such from you. I can manage. No need to worry on my account."

"Nonetheless, I feel you may have had enough of people on this day. Do you ever sell to the keep kitchens?"

Milly's eyes grew wide as she shook her head, as if she would never do such a thing. "Is there a reason you cannot sell to the castle?"

She bit her lip but shook her head no.

"Very well. You shall go to the castle kitchens and ask for Palle. She is the head chef. Take her this handkerchief. She will recognize it. Tell her I request she purchase all your eggs today and set a schedule to buy eggs from you at least once a week from today on. I will confirm all myself when I return to the keep."

I handed Milly the handkerchief from inside my sleeve, a delicate cream linen with the crest of Lady Ingar embroidered on one corner. She stared at it a moment before turning a beaming smile my way and thanking me profusely. I shooed her on her way, sent another glare to the men who tormented her, and was about to launch into a lecture when I saw them smile a little too broadly. Then I felt a strong, cold hand clamp down like a vise on my shoulder. Someone tugged at me aggressively and I spun on my heels, startled and alert. Codiff stood over me, haughty as always, peering down his nose and sucking his teeth.

"I see, despite your upbringing, you require further instruction on decorum. My lady, it is inappropriate for you to talk to one such as her."

"Why is that?" I asked.

Codiff's gaze narrowed at my question. It was the first time I'd ever questioned him. Or willingly engaged him in what could be considered conversation. Clearly he did not want anyone to question him, a man of great authority in this place. However, I genuinely wished to know what he had meant. Was I not the Lady of Ingar, tasked with caring for the people in this land?

"She is beneath you in station, and as the two guards at your back informed me while you bickered with the men sent to protect you, she is known as a woman of ill repute."

"Is it not my duty to mingle with all in the market? The specific reason why Lord Ingar asked me to venture outside the castle this day?" I pulled myself up, finding strength in the anger I felt at his answer. Yet I knew what I should say in the moment rather than giving vent to all I wished to say. I didn't question the other assertions—the idea she was a woman or possibly had a sordid reputation. One was beneath my concern and arguably untrue and unkind.

The other was a blatant lie, whether these men recognized it or not. She was but a girl, and one in need of protection.

My ire gave me courage and surety where I had found none for the past months in Ingar. For too long I had hung back, still new to Ingar and its ways, its people. Sadly, in this discourse, I was not new. I understood what whispers could do to a female, true or false, and how easily force girls to become women. Even if I remained protected from certain levels of advances as a lord's daughter and was still more protected from the accosting of strangers as a lord's wife, I had seen it happen enough in my short life. It took but simple words and quick actions in stolen moments to devastate a girl like Milly, or even a woman like myself.

"You are new to our land, Lady Roselle," Master Codiff began, but I cut him off quickly.

"True. And I am well aware you attempt to... educate me in the ways of this place. I appreciate the act of kindness. I do, however, have sense enough to understand today's events. I stepped in because it was proper and just to do so. As Lady of these lands, justice should be at the forefront of my mind, wouldn't you agree?"

Now seething, unable to imagine a world where I questioned him, much less did not allow him to fully vent his speech, the mage's hands fisted at his sides, pulsing to the rhythm of his anger. It sparked fear in me, but my own indignation rose like a flame to meet it, devour it, giving me strength enough to match his stare with a calmness that seemed to make his face turn more and more crimson by the second.

"You know not what you do, young lady," he hissed, losing his mask of civility.

"It is Lady Roselle of Ingar Keep, even to one such as you, mage," I calmly asserted while holding his simmering gaze. We stared for a long moment, him breathing heavier than normal, me a calm exterior masking a war of fear and anger inside my own breast.

He was the first to break our gaze, and a flash in his eyes told me it cost him dearly to do so. But if I knew anything of men like this, I knew it would also cost me something in the future. The question became would it be a high or low cost, a cost worth the outcome. For now I imagined so; no real price the mage could extract would have made it not worth helping out the poor girl.

After gazing at his feet for a few beats, enough to collect and compose his mask, he looked at me sharply, quick enough that I only caught the ghost of a snarl on his lips. When he gave a curt nod and small bow to depart, he swept his robes aside and looked back to pose a parting question. "I wonder…what Lord Ingar will say of your actions this day?"

"As do I," I countered, heat in my words and my stare at his implied threat. My husband was a kind man, but a man who ruled. While I hoped he would understand, there was always the chance of disappointment.

I stood tall and watched the mage blend back into the shadows. He looked, watched, waited, and had reacted, and he would report back all he saw. I knew this before. Now, however, with the sizzle of indignation pumping through my veins, I did not hesitate at this thought but moved forward, firm in the knowledge that what I had done for Milly was good and right. Affirming my rightful place with the mage was the proper action, even if the small battle meant a later war.

The guards grumbled slightly, but my hard face made them stop their mouths. Their faces, however, showed their full displeasure as they crowded together in my wake, staying well behind the person they should be protecting. The ladies-in-waiting reappeared for a moment, whispering to themselves, curtseying and asking if I was in need. I dismissed them, rebuffing all attempts at conversation for the time being. They also soon fell back, leaving me to lead with no one at my side, strolling through the

thoroughfare looking this way and that, studying for anything that caught my attention or
anyone who looked to be in need. I stopped
only when I heard the sharp cry of my name
from an unknown voice.

Six

A few lanes down from my confrontation with the guards and the mage, I heard a loud, clear voice call out. "Lady Ingar. Please, do grace my stall with your presence."

She was the first to call upon me in the market. Everyone else hung back, waiting for my approach. When I peered toward the voice, I saw an older woman, gray and stooped, wearing a shimmering yellow dress. I stood mesmerized, as if staring at sunshine spun into fabric, and I moved toward her. She curtseyed as best she could and craned her neck up to look in my face. There, for the second time in a short span, I looked deep into golden-orange eyes.

I gasped and she laughed. "Family trait my granddaughter was burdened with, my lady."

"I would not call such a burden," I said, staring into the depth of those eyes. Often, people looked away when I studied them—their lines and color and planes. I knew it was rude, but it was an artistic impulse when something fascinated me. This woman, however, did not budge. She didn't even blink. She stared back with a quiet certainty and confidence I envied. It was I who looked away first this time, finding her gaze too much.

Her kind and knowing look turned bitter when she spotted my guards stopped in the center of the thoroughfare, blocking traffic and laughing while keeping half their attention on me, the one they were supposed to be guarding. Turning to go deeper into her stall, she said, "I believe, after what transpired earlier, you know I speak truth."

I nodded, saddened and chastised both. "I am sorry," I stated.

"No, my lady. You owe no one an apology. I, however, owe you thanks."

When she moved to round a small table, I finally looked away and noticed her wares. Hidden in the dark of the stall were mounds and mounds of various fabrics, a riot of rich color. I ran my fingers along a bolt of deep red that bordered on black, struck by the way it shimmered, much like the yellow of the old woman's gown.

"Do you create these fabrics?"

"Aye. That I do. With a few select apprentices."

"Why have I never seen them before?" I muttered, more to myself as I moved to look at an ivory cloth practically glistening in the soft light filtering into the tent.

"My family does not have the best reputation in this town, as you may have heard. I suspect many believe we are not good enough to serve a lady such as yourself."

I pulled up and asked, "What is your name?"

"I am Andra, my lady," she said with a smaller, swifter curtsey. "A true pleasure to have you in my simple stall."

"I wish to buy this ivory bolt," I declared after a brief acknowledgement of her courteousness. "Also, do you sell thread? Thick enough for weaving tapestries?"

She nodded and moved me toward a box lined with the most beautiful, shimmering cords of thread in a rainbow of colors. I picked out an armful without hesitation. After calling my attending ladies forward, I offloaded my wares while they heaved heavy sighs and cut sharp looks at Andra. It is likely they would also have words with Lord Ingar about my associations. I did not care.

I was about to bid the old woman farewell when a flash of lavender stopped me in my tracks. A few loose yards of fabric haphazardly decorated the wall of the stall. Peeking out from one side was a purple so like the dragon's eyes that I immediately froze and narrowed my focus on it. Reaching out to shove the others away, I saw it was a small section, no more than a hand length long. It was useless in practical sense, but the color so matched the eyes that haunted my thoughts, it felt like it could not be coincidence.

"I see you find the last bit of that color I have. I wish I had more to offer. Sadly, it is hard to come by and often taken much too soon."

"It reminds me..."

"Of one you saw last night? I imagine it does. I heard the tale already myself."

"Are all their eyes this color?"

"No, my lady. Dragon eyes come in many shades, just as dragon skin. Just as people."

"I wish I'd seen them alive," I said on a quiet whisper, giving voice to something I hadn't yet fully admitted to myself.

"A sight few humans are allowed to see, but a beautiful one indeed. Dragons' eyes glow and blaze in their own right because fire fills their being."

Drawn in even more now, I asked, "You've seen a live dragon?"

"Aye. I have, my lady. I've lived a long life and have seen much mystery and magic."

"Were you afraid?" I continued, needing to know the experience, wanting answers to push away my dreams.

"No, my lady." She gave a huff, exasperated, before she bit out, "There are many things the world of men does not understand. The lack of understanding leads to conjecture, to fear, to hate."

"You sound as if you speak from experience, Andra."

"Experience with dragons, with my own life and ways, Lady Ingar." She turned away from me, moved to straighten a bolt of fabric, and in a low voice, asked, "Does my honesty frighten you?"

I stopped. Thought. It was a serious conversation, one I wished to have to help me learn, but I felt Andra deserved honesty. I was hesitant, yes. The hesitancy, however, did not come from fear of what she said to me, what she might be implying about herself and magic and dragons. The fear was in learning too much, not liking what I would find in the new knowledge. Yet I had a need to push forward, think through these inconsistencies, and dig into a different truth. After several beats, the time to truly consider and align my thoughts, I replied, "No, Andra. I do not fear you or what you say. I wish to hear more, if you are willing."

"Always willing, my lady. Yet there is another you should discuss such with."

Blaine flashed in my mind and I nodded, knowing I needed to know what he knew, what he was aware of, what he acted on when out on a hunt. "I must speak with my husband," I said firmly, moving to leave on that very errand.

Andra gave me an encouraging smile, the wrinkles on her face deepening as she did, showing laugh and worry lines etched into her face over the years. "Please do return, my lady. For more fabric or conversation. It is good for an old woman to tell what she knows from time to time."

I nodded absentmindedly and walked away, leaving the market entirely. On a mission to find out more from my husband about his hunt.

Seven

I RARELY ENTERED MY husband's study. One very practical reason was Lord Ingar was rarely in the study himself. He preferred more hands-on pursuits such as training, meetings over food and drink, or discussions while enjoying another activity like walking or riding. He was an action-oriented man, and the study was a place of quiet and stillness. When necessity forced him into the room, it was usually by meetings with his overseer or legal advisors or even, occasionally, Codiff. Hence the second reason I rarely entered: it was a place my husband discussed or thought through matters he felt to be of no concern to me.

I was not barred from the room, or even outwardly discouraged from entering the space. I had visited my husband a handful of times when he had been alone reviewing correspondence or tracking the numbers that allowed his small corner of the world to prosper. He had always greeted me with a warm smile on those occasions.

This day, however, I was told by a footman Lord Ingar had requested my presence in his study. I instructed my ladies-in-waiting to carry the fabrics and thread purchased at Andra's stall directly to my workroom. I doled out the rest of my purchases to various servants as I shook off the dust and disappointment of the day and put on a smile for Blaine.

When I approached, I saw Codiff for the first time since our confrontation in the market. He exited the study with a stiff spine, turning curtly away from me and gliding farther down the opposite end of the hallway. I knew better than to assume he did not see me or notice my approach. The mage was too observant for that. He noted me, had likely even waited for my arrival before leaving, giving me a subtle rebuff, showing me he had whispered in my husband's ear. What would occur next was all based on what Codiff had said in my absence. My hope was he would also listen to my voice.

I knocked, and when Blaine's deep voice called, I entered. He was sitting, looking down at a stack of scrolls on his desk, forehead furrowed in thought, before toward me with a soft sigh I barely heard, a sigh that sounded a lot like light annoyance.

"Wife." He stood and moved to take my hands.

I gave a small dip of my knees, and he offered sweeping kisses to my cheeks. My face heated slightly at the caress of his touch.

Pulling back to stare down at me from a few feet away, he said, "I have heard concerning things about your outing this morning."

"I am sure you have, although I am still at a loss as to why my actions upset Master Codiff so," I replied, hoping to get the facts out in the open. I wanted Blaine to know I was aware of Codiff's displeasure and the fact he was the one to discuss such things with my husband, but I also wanted to remain firm in my assertion that I did no wrong in helping Milly.

"My dear, sweet, naive Roselle." He sighed, lifting a hand to rub my cheek. "According to Codiff, the woman you spoke with has a certain reputation."

"Husband, I understand the reservation. Yet, often, women's reputations are unwarranted. I must be frank. Milly was a girl terrorized by my guard. A girl of no more than fourteen, if that. She has not lived enough life to warrant any reputation based on her own actions or garner any attention from the guards of this land, much less the aggressive and menacing way they were treating her this morning."

"You have such a kind heart, wife. It makes you a thoughtful and caring Lady Ingar. Still, prudence is always required. I honestly know nothing of this Milly save what you and Codiff say, and each tells a slightly different version of events. The core, however, is still true, yes? You berated your guard and argued with Master Codiff?"

"I would not say so. I would say I stopped your guard from injuring a girl in the presence of your people and I calmly countered Codiff's reproach."

"Perspectives differ, surely. I do know that you, as a woman and an artist, can be emotional..." He trailed off and I hung my head. Not in shame. I hid the heat of the anger and disappointment rising in my face. Blaine still knew so little of me. We were still so new to each other, but to have him assume and practically side with Codiff in this was a blow to my trust and affection for him.

"Yet, I know you to be wise, even when following your heart," he said, finally finishing after a few beats. "You try to help, and that is commendable."

My disappointment abated some, but the sting was a memory I kept tucked away. "What would you have had me do?" I asked, genuinely curious.

"Be gentler in your approach to the guards and the mage. Rely on your kindness and heart, not your anger, and you will endear yourself to these men. They wish only to protect and guide, to save you from any harm—be it physical or related to your own reputation."

I nodded, not agreeing but taking a bit of his advice in the moment and being agreeable with my husband. I imagined, with time and familiarity, our bond would strengthen. He would come to trust me and I him. That is what would change the dynamic of my life in this place, not deferring to guards or Codiff. Before it could happen, I needed more knowledge: of him, of this place, and of the lavender-eyed dragon.

"You say you do not know of Milly. Do you know of her grandmother, Andra? I also met her today. Purchased lovely fabric and thread from her stall in the market."

"Ah, yes. Old Andra." Blaine chuckled. "Old, it seems, even when I was a child. Her artistry is impeccable, sought out by many. Which is the sole reason why she remains here in Ingar and has not been driven out."

"Driven out?"

"Yes." Blaine sighed, pulling me closer, into the circle of his arms. "See, Little Light, this is why you must heed the warnings of Codiff. We tolerate Andra because of her talents. However, there have long been whispers of witchcraft and magic connected to her."

Confused, I declared, "The mage uses magic."

"There is a difference," Blaine said, his tone like a teacher lecturing an errant pupil. "Mages learn magic from long study and toil. Only certain men with vast ability can achieve the title of master. Witchcraft, the magic a woman like that would wield, is more wild and unruly, and therefore forbidden because of its inherent danger."

"Like the magic of dragons?" I pushed, hoping for more information.

Blaine stared at me a beat, taking a moment to decide what he would say. "Perhaps similar, in that both are destructive to our way of life. Dragons, however, are born creatures bent of magic and destruction. Witches are merely led astray, seduced by a magic and a power they should never access."

"Why?" I asked again, as if I were a child learning anew. I was, in some respects. I wished to think to the bottom, dig into the reasoning behind these assumptions Blaine spewed. Ones I had also learned years before from my guardian and tutors.

"It is not for you to ask why, Little Light," he said with an indulgent smile before bending down to kiss away my protestations, my thoughts. "Instead of questioning, you must focus on remaining a proper lady at all times, in and out of our keep. Your kind intentions do not matter if your actions smear your name. What others say of us becomes reality, wife, and I will not have you besmirched for the benefit of some wayward woman."

I stepped back from him, turning my head to yet again hide my pain and disappointment at his attitude, his overall dismissal, at what he had said outright and what he had implied with his choice of words. Blaine's hands pulled at my hips, bringing me into his chest. He gave me a powerful hug while bending to kiss the top of my head. It was all sweetness, and for a second, I wanted to push away what I'd heard and focus on all that was good. However, no woman survived if she ignored bad signs and omens, and I knew a little of the tangle of omens and memory. Enough that when the dreams returned later that night, they sparked something more in me.

Eight

Thoughts crowded my head while Blaine snored next to me, his heavy arm slung across my belly in a soft grip. We talked little of what I learned, what I thought, in general. This day had been no different, even if I learned a great deal about the world and my husband's ideas about it. When I finally drifted off to sleep, my last thought was of my mother, long gone—so long gone, the ache I still felt surprised me whenever it squeezed my heart.

Perhaps it was why I dreamed so ferociously again. It started with a shock of blood, a clang of swords. A cave I did not recognize hovered in mist and smoke, a gray and cold carving out of mountain. I heard a scream echo in its depths. Next came a flash of memory, highlighting lavender eyes on a banquet table, its shifting skin of scales turning into a kaleidoscope of color. I reached for the head to offer comfort, to close its dead eyes, but it remained out of my grasp, no matter how hard I stretched and moved to get at the poor creature. A cackle of deep laughter filled the air, and I caught Codiff staring from the other side of the table, one hand wrapped in chain, the other clutching the remnants of a fine blue fabric. Hate spilled out, a physical thing made of deep, dark shadows in my dream state. I reared back and looked about frantically for my husband. He stood at the other end of the table, a jolly expression on his face, offered a wink toward me, a smile at Codiff, then a turn back to laughs and roars with his guards and friends. When he moved away, it felt like a snapping of strings from an unknown tether in my gut.

A swirl of time and place and I hovered outside myself, watching as I was again in the market, again at Andra's stall, caressing the lavender fabric. It shone in the dream light, its own color shifting and changing like it was not solid cloth but rather a tapestry intricately woven with a multiplicity of shimmering threads so small and interconnected it was impossible to see where one began and another ended. I watched myself pull it close to my nose and breathe deep as if comforted. Glancing over into the shadowed recessed of the booth, I saw Andra stare at the me among her fabrics and threads. She shook her head before looking up, as if seeing the me who hovered somewhere on the periphery of this reality, her deep-golden eyes flashing in recognition and knowledge. With a blink I moved from my out-of-body position apart from the scene to viewing the dream world through my singular perspective. I was in my body, seeing from my body in the stall, staring back into Andra's eyes now so close to my own.

"Remember," dream Andra whispered to me.

I tried to ask her questions, tried to understand what I was to remember, but my voice didn't come. Instead of sound, smoke fell from my mouth in gray waves, curling into the air and hanging between us. I rubbed my throat, then clawed. I screamed, but more and more smoke spilled out in place of sound, filling the space between us and obscuring my vision. Andra acted unconcerned. She reached for my hand, pulling it down from my windpipe, and gave it a soft squeeze. "Remember," she whispered again before she and the stall and I all melted away in a swirl of smoke that turned darker and hotter. Shot through with spark and ember, the smoke churned, creaked, and groaned, and suddenly, all was aflame. A woman's cry pierced the crackling and roaring of the fire. My mother's cry. I jolted up in bed, drenched in sweat as if too close to the burning in my dream, my heart pounding and my mind racing.

Quietly and gently rising from bed so as to not disturb Blaine, I moved to the water jug, poured the crystalline liquid into the basin, and dunked my entire face into the cool depths, hoping to wash the vivid visuals from my mind as I washed the sweat from my brow. I pulled up when my lungs screamed for breath. Grabbing a linen from the stand, I moved slowly from the basin and took a seat on one of the wooden chairs that flanked the dying fire. I stared at the embers, thought of my dream, and started when I remembered my mother's cry.

It was unfamiliar in many ways. My mother had lived a happy life with my father as lady of our lands, though I knew she had not been born to expect such a life. A commoner by birth, she learned the role of a lady much later in life. My father had spied her one day during some youthful travels and fell easily in love. He married her without concern for tradition or protocol and brought her to his small keep, making her his lady. Despite, or maybe because of this, the people in our small realm respected and loved her. She had little reason to cry out in alarm during her life in our home. Yet, there had been one time when this had happened, and for the life of me, I could not fathom how

I had forgotten it. A childhood memory, one of the few hard memories for me, somehow had burrowed itself so deeply into my mind, I had not recalled it until Andra had urged me in my dream to remember. It was the sole time I had heard my mother cry out in rage or devastation.

It was the spring of my eighth year, less than six months before I lost both of my parents. The frost had recently subsided, and small buds popped here and there in and around our keep. My father was a lord, his own holding in the Midlands far from the southern edges of Ingar lands, though it had been a small track compared to what my husband held. It was beautiful however, all lush deep-green forest and dark-brown earth. Rolling hills dotted the distance in most vistas. Spring came early, while summer lingered longer because of an odd quirk in our position.

My early childhood was filled with happiness, for the most part. As with everyone, there were small moments of pain or anger or frustration. My father loved me fiercely and never acted disappointed my mother had never given him a son. Mother doted but did not spoil. She allowed me to stumble when it was prudent, punished me when necessary, and encouraged me often. I was sheltered, true, but not completely. If I was anything, it was appropriately prepared. My parents did not hide goings-on in the castle, as they both hoped I would run my own one day. That would require knowledge and experience from an early age. I saw much I did not understand until I was older, and I was sometimes even frightened by events, but I learned much in the brief years I spent in my homeland with my family.

My parents also loved one another, a fact both Mother and Father claimed and an idea Mother emphasized. They were a love match, and although Father had planned on arranging my marriage, he had hesitated to do so when I was younger. It was an unusual move, and one reason my guardians so hastily arranged my betrothal to Blaine. Ladies were most often given in marriage as infants, and my guardian informed me I was lucky a family as prestigious and strong as the Ingar's were in search of an older girl for their heir.

It was not a concern for my parents, however, as they had wanted to give me a chance at love because they loved. Fiercely. They rarely fought, never raised voices to one another—in my hearing at least—and valued and respected each other in a way that made it the norm in our land. They kissed, touched, and held each other often. They encouraged this behavior in all around them. My father railed against any guards or men he knew that did not treat their women with what he felt was appropriate respect. My mother was quick to point such instances out to him if she perceived an issue. They felt deeply for each other, showed it in word and deed, and expected courtesy at a bare minimum for all in similar relationships, regardless of rank or position.

This was why the echo of a rage-filled scream had startled me so that day. It was dusk, almost time for supper, and Father was long away with a party of other lords in our lands doing who-knew-what. He was supposed to be home that evening, which was why I had my ear trained for the door. Also why my mother, on the sight of what he carried in with him, immediately reacted. She was waiting for his return in the hall closest to the entryway.

I ran. There was nothing else to do. My mind couldn't comprehend what I heard, so I bolted to the source in an effort to see, to help if needed. Surely something dire had occurred to make my mother bellow out such a mournful and angry sound. As I neared, I heard Mother's raised voice, high and tight with a mixture of anger and pain that made me quake and ache at the same time. I heard Father's deep rumble, calm and attempting to soothe.

As I reached the final darkened arch that would take me to my parents, I stopped. I hesitated. Instead of running fully into the room, I crept forward, peeking my small head around the edge of the stone frame to glimpse what was there.

My mother was no longer yelling. It was worse. She was on the floor weeping ugly, gasping tears. My father stood over her, misery and hesitancy and guilt written clearly on his face. Before Mother, spread across her knees, was a bejeweled length of hide. Skin with a shimmer whenever it shifted in the light. It was dragon skin, worked as a trophy or showpiece for a wall mount. It was not massive, but it was substantial. Mother stroked her hands along it, making a choking noise as she did.

"Did you hunt..." Her words were hard and biting to my ears, so much so that I flinched at the same time Father did.

"Of course not, Corine. How could you ask such of me?" he replied, hurt and offended by the question I did not understand.

"I never thought I would. Never imagined. Until you bring this to our home. The home you share with me and your daughter."

"I am so sorry, my love." He tried to place a hand on her shoulder. She wrenched herself away and looked back at him. The blaze of her blue eyes, eyes so similar to my own, struck fear in me—for Father, for Mother, for myself. There was a literal spark there, something strong and dangerous and unlike anything I had ever seen in another's look.

"Why? WHY!?" she screamed.

"Love, please. Listen. Listen. I sent a messenger to warn you, but, sadly, they did not arrive before me. I could not dismiss or deny the gift without cause, without revealing too much to those men. More than that, I knew after your initial shock and grief you would want to mourn. Observe your rites."

Mother, still crying, kneeled back down to the skin and muttered words I didn't understand. She studied it, tears streaming down her face, then pulled herself up while heaving deep breaths in and out. She was calmer when she spoke next, even if she did not look at my father when she spoke.

"It was a tragic miscommunication then. Understandable. Regrettable. You must, however, give me time to recover. I need to deal with my loss, honor the dead, and meet the fire on my own."

"Yes, Corine." Father answered quickly, pity and sadness and reverence mixed in his broken tone. "Do as you will. I will be here when you return."

Mother scooped up the jeweled hide and walked swiftly out the door, dismissing all attendants who attempted to follow. She took no coat, no supplies, nothing but the hide, and she did not return until morning. It was the only night, until her death, she had not tucked me into my bed. When Father turned to see me, crouched and rigid with fear, he scooped me up, held me close in a fierce grip, and muttered his own words of regret and love and sadness. Words I didn't understand. Words of protection that made no sense to me, as a child or as Lady Ingar, but words that still echo in my bones.

Nine

I had to leave my bedchamber. I felt stuck in there, hemmed in by memory and Blaine's soft snores. I threw on a nightrobe and quietly left, making sure the door was slightly ajar to not disturb my husband's sleep when I returned. Padding swiftly down the hallway, mindless in a way, I eventually brought myself to the one place I was most at ease in the keep. I knew a fire would burn in the hearth to keep the temperatures running for the kitchen's daily use, so I expected a small measure of comfort and warmth. From other late-night wanders, I also knew I might find a stray biscuit or cookie in the storage cupboard. I didn't dare take anything Pelle would miss in the morning during these late-night trips. No matter my status, I knew she would have no qualms railing at me for missing reserved sweets, as my sweet tooth would make me the most likely culprit.

To my surprise, there were soft noises coming from the kitchen, and a more substantial fire glowed. I entered to find Palle in her uniform, covered in more soot than normal. This was due to her activity: Palle was scouring cast-iron kettles. An array of them, in various stages of curing, took up the workbench. I startled at the sight when I entered, and Palle offered me a tired but genuine grin in turn.

"Another late-night trip for sweets, my lady? Lord Ingar must keep you ravenous in the night then." She chuckled at her joke, and I ducked my head, not in shame at the innuendo but in embarrassment that it wasn't exactly true.

"Bad dreams," I muttered, chewing my lip as I took a seat on my stool.

Palle paused and studied my face, her own softening. "Is that why you're in my kitchens so often at night?"

Deciding to deflect the question, I asked my own. "How do you know how often I'm here?"

She nodded and let me have my evasions. "My lady, a speck of dust can't be out of place in these rooms without me knowing about it. I know every nook and cranny, every stain, every crumb before I put myself in my room for the night. Can always tell when you've sat there, whether I see you with my own eyes or not."

Knowing this to be true, the attention and care she gave her kitchens, I said no more, just scanned the room before coming back and asking her, "Why do you work so late this evening?"

"Bah. These old pots need curing, and I only trust myself to do it right. Do this every so often to keep them all in working order, and there's too much to do in the day to make time for it then. So night it is."

"Would you like help?" I whispered, hesitant but eager, thinking maybe some work would help clear my mind and lead me to rest.

"Oh, no thank you, Lady Ingar. Our lord is much kinder and sweeter than his predecessor, for certain, yet I do believe he'd give me a thrashing if he learned I let you scrub pots in the dead of night."

"Blaine is not here. He is sleeping soundly above with no idea I'm even in the kitchens."

Palle gave me a soft smile then, something warmer but also sadder than the normal grin I was so used to seeing. "And sorry for that I am, my lady. Does Lord Ingar often sleep soundly?"

I knew she asked for my sake, coming back around to the issues of dreams, so I gave her a tentative answer. "More soundly than I."

Turning her head to make sure she oiled every spot of the large kettle between her worn hands, she muttered, "As is the way with men with no need to fret. They sleep well, with few dreams."

I only nodded, and she allowed the conversation to drop. I sat while she worked, long minutes passing without us speaking. The quiet comfort of being with a woman I respected and liked chased away the dream and the dark memories it held. However, questions loomed, and if I could ask anyone in the keep, I knew I could ask Palle.

"Do you know much of dragons?" I blurted finally.

Palle jumped slightly at the speed of the random question, the echo of my voice in the quiet kitchen. She paused, thought some before offering a reply. "Not much save what all learn, I suppose. Other whispers here and there. Anything in particular you wish to know?"

I had asked but felt uncomfortable pushing her, my only friend—even if I couldn't actually call her a friend because of our positions and place in Ingar Keep. I simply shrugged and muttered about dreams.

"Dreams are special, my lady. Don't forget them. They might tell you something."

"My mother used to say something similar," I admitted.

"Likely a smart lady herself."

"She died when I was very young," I said, still raw from the memories the dream brought back to me, the ache I held, would likely always hold, for a mother lost to me.

"Aye. I remember talk of it, before and after your betrothal to Lord Ingar." She left it at that, not prying when I did not offer more.

More silence passed, comfortable but heavy after our last burst of conversation. Palle waded in again, softly asking, "At the market, did you happen to buy fabrics or thread?"

I perked up at this, though I only answered, "Yes."

"From Andra?"

When I jerked my head to affirm, my body stiff with surprise at the direction of the conversation, Palle resumed scrubbing with a bit of chainmail, muttering almost to herself.

"She's also a smart woman. One with lots of answers to lots of questions."

She'd shown up in my dream, and now she was here between me and Palle, her name lighting up my mind, sending questions spiraling. I decided to see her next market day. Palle's hints made me more eager for that to happen. Even she believed Andra could help me with whatever it was about my past, my present, these questions of dragons that continued to haunt me.

"Quite true," I muttered, blinking at my hands in my lap. I stared there for long moments before realizing I'd become sleepier than I thought. Deciding to take my leave from Palle and the comfort of the kitchens, to head back to my bedchamber in the hope of a dreamless sleep, I heaved myself from the stool with a sigh and simply said, "Good night, Palle."

As I shuffled from the room, pulling my robe tighter around me in anticipation of the cold, empty halls ahead, I turned to leave but stopped short when Palle called, "Lady Ingar?"

I looked back at the cook bent deep into the recess of the hearth, arranging kettles so they dried evenly.

She did not look up at me as she said, "The eggs you procured are working quite nicely." With a deep breath she continued, quiet enough I had to lean forward to make sure I heard clearly. "Milly girl has had a difficult life in Ingar, as her mother and grandmother before her. It is sad, to see one so young so mistreated, by men and women alike."

She looked at me then, her piercing brown eyes showing kindness and keenness in turn, as she stated, "You did right by her. May not be my place to say, but I wished to say it nonetheless. You continue to do right in such a way, you may just leave a more lasting mark on this world than you imagine."

She looked back at her kettles, as if she hadn't spoken words that saw through the heart of me, as if she hadn't pierced me with talk of goodness and righteousness. With legacy and marks. I blinked after her a moment, pulled myself up, and allowed her words to wrap around me, a blanket of sorts. A comforting shield. The mage and my husband had derided me for my actions. I knew I had been right, but it felt good for someone I respected and liked to say I had done right.

I nodded, even though Palle was turned away, and left the kitchen. Eyes and fire and smoke did not follow me as I made my way to the bedchamber, as they had in my dreams before. Instead, I walked the chilled halls of the keep with a soft burn in my heart at the kindness and approval of Palle, at the assurance of what I had done and what I could still do as Lady Roselle Ingar—if I had more time and a few more answers.

TEN

I waited patiently for the next market day, working in a distracted manner on my tapestry. It served a two-fold purpose: mind and body enjoyed the work, and the use of more thread necessitated another visit to Andra's stall. An unnecessary pretext perhaps, but I was cautious in my approach with the fabric monger. Her appearance in my dream felt all too real. The memory it had triggered in me seemed connected to current events beyond mere coincidence. I needed answers she may be able to give, and something whispered in my mind I needed a reason to be in her stall, talking with her.

The singular blessing of the long days before market was I often found myself lost in my art, the shimmer and shine of my thread and the feel of it as it ran across my fingers. The pull of the needle was a repetitive comfort.

When not at my stand, staring into my design, pulling it forward with steel and fabric, I focused on Andra, my husband, my dreams, and my memory. Formulating ideas and hypotheses I did not dare share with anyone. Not yet. I put on smiles when necessary, even had a few genuine smiles during this time. I laughed at Blaine's jokes, flushed at his kisses, smiled at tales and news shared in the banquet hall. Always, though, in the back of my head, what I thought I knew lurked, ready to thread through my waking thoughts and turning my mind to the unanswered questions I had.

Finally, market day came. I wandered the rows, not immediately heading to Andra. It was a hard thing, to meander when I had a destination in mind. It was also deceptive, an act of forethought that made my meeting with the woman feel both necessary and clandestine.

The guards lingered behind me at a safe distance, and the ladies-in-waiting whispered and fluttered closer to me, even occasionally attempting conversation. They had softened to me in the past week and were attempting to engage. It may have been paranoia on my part, but I strongly suspected they were doing such at the behest of my husband and not in any true attempt to befriend me. They were artful and practiced in their graces, something I could respect as a woman also raised to be a lady. Their practiced ways were part of who they were, what their position was. I knew this. My mind and heart told me these women were true to my husband and his concerns, not me and mine, and as such could not count as confidants. Divided loyalties do not cement friendships.

I purchased soap and meats, various trinkets here and there, and kept watch on the guards in case another incident transpired. They laughed and joked, appearing mostly distracted and not effective in their charge. Yet they did not harass anyone, and they continued in my sight the entire day, not breaking off into a smaller group or leaving me to wander on my own. It was part blessing and part curse, as I knew someone would report whatever I did to another, be it my husband or Codiff. The guards were sharp and observant when they had a mind to it, and the longer I lingered in the market, the more assured I was in my previous caution. Now, as I reached the fabric stall in at a seemingly natural pace, I doubted they would concern themselves with the matter.

The stall stood as it had before, fabric gently sweeping in the soft breeze, an arrangement of tables piled with wares, and shadows in the depths. Hoping to find Andra inside, I stepped farther in, pushing my way through a beautiful blue satin fabric that reminded me of delicate bird eggs. The old woman sat in a corner on a rugged wooden stool. Upon my entrance, she pulled herself upright with the help of a knobby, dark wooden cane and flashed her keen golden eyes at me before attempting a curtsey.

"My lady," she said, trying to bend her knees to show her respect.

I rushed forward, halting her with a firm hand on her upper arm. "No, Andra. Please. Do not bend your body for me. I am perfectly happy to leave such formalities behind."

She gave a slight nod and offered a broad smile. "As you wish, Lady Ingar. What a kind lady you prove to be, in all things. Do you mind if I sit? My bones are weary this day. More so than usual, for some reason."

"Yes. Please do. I come to buy more thread. For my tapestry. You need not stand."

"Only for thread?" she asked, her head tilted with the question.

"Not only, no," I admitted. I could not bring myself to look at the woman then, so I instead turned toward the thread in question, stroking bundles and picking out the most vibrant shades for my work. Color and softness filled my hands and I gazed down at it, a marvel of fabric, before I whispered, "I dreamed the other night."

"You can learn much in dreams." The old woman hummed, plucking the threads from my hand and gently wrapping them in thick paper stacked beside her stool.

"As my mother always said," I replied, finally meeting her sharp and knowing gaze.

"A wise woman, no doubt."

"As many women are."

"Yes. True. Though some would not wish us to say as much," she replied with a rueful smile.

I swallowed, about to ask more and dig deeper, when she waved a finger between us. It was a subtle movement, one I noticed offhandedly, but it was enough to stop my tongue right before I heard a familiar throat clearing behind me.

I turned and found Codiff carefully watching me and Andra. He greeted me with a sweep of his hand and a small half bow. "Lady Ingar."

"Master Codiff," I replied, stiff in my posture. I was happy to be between him and Andra, happy to spare her the bulk of his withering, judgmental gaze.

I studied the stall and fingered a piece of heavy navy linen hanging by his head, a color so rich and deep, it mimicked the night sky to perfection. "Purchasing more fabric? So soon?"

"Threads, actually," I replied, turning toward Andra to retrieve the filled bundle. "I need more for my grand tapestry."

"Ah, yes. This great artistic work of yours. Soon to grace our keep."

I bristled at the mocking tone of his words but said nothing. I stared instead, steady and unblinking, into his face. The longer I looked on him without speaking, the stonier his face became, as if my daring to silently stare was a grave insult. The animosity I felt from him, the disrespect that radiated in palpable waves, was something I was unused to in my life. My thoughts had been of home often over the week, and as I lingered in my memory, the way Codiff treated me became more and more unbearable. How I ignored it before was a mystery, but I was, at that point, finished with ignoring the mage.

"Do you wish to speak of something, Master Codiff? Or possibly purchase some fabric for your own use?" I asked, questioning his presence before me in a way he could not misinterpret.

"No, my lady," he answered, offering no more. Standing firm, he telegraphed he would not budge from his position in the stall until I also moved along.

"Very well. I am done here," I said, sending a look to Andra in hopes she would understand why I left so hastily. She was bent over a thin bit of paper wrapping on her lap, seemingly paying little attention to the exchange.

However, when I moved to pay her, she pushed herself straight and asked, "Did you wish to also buy the blue satin you discussed earlier?" Her hands moved over the paper in her lap, a soft caress bringing my gaze down to barely visible markings there. She'd written something to me, wanted me to take it from the stall.

"Yes. As I said earlier, the blue satin as well. Enough for a new banquet dress. I believe eight yards should suffice."

"Such an astute and kindly merchant," the mage said in a bland yet mocking tone.

Andra ignored his words and moved to retrieve the bolt, but I stopped her. No need for her to rise from her stool. I shifted to gather the fabric and saw Codiff had already stepped close. He held the bolt in his hand out toward me as one finger gently stroked the material.

"Allow me, my lady," he said, sliding the fabric around my body, leaning over enough to stare hard at Andra as he handed over the section of cloth. She took the material from his grip without looking up, focusing on the fabric as she measured out yard by yard on a small space close to her stool. She wrapped it tight, first with the faintly marked paper, then with more to obscure any writing. In the end, I paid for my tidy bundles—one of thread, one of satin—and forced my eyes away from the packages, not wanting to hint at any possible importance to the mage.

"After you, Lady Roselle," he boomed, throwing his arm out toward the lane.

I nodded and swept past. He kept pace, occasionally commenting as I entered other stalls and made additional purchases or talked with other vendors. He never left my side while I wandered the rest of the market, forcing me to wait until much later to read the message secreted to me by Andra between folds of soft, slick blue satin the color of a bright, clear sky.

Eleven

After dismissing my ladies-in-waiting, claiming I needed time for rest after a long morning in the market, I secreted the bundle of blue satin cloth into my rooms. Blaine never entered the bedchambers in the day. He was always off attending to people or business or other pursuits. I sat on the rug before a low-lit fire and carefully unwrapped the package, taking care to not damage the delicate paper message. In the flicker of firelight, the hand was faint yet clear. It simply read: "Milly. Service stairway outside kitchens. Midafternoon." It was a rendezvous then, a meeting with Milly.

I told myself I was being overly cautious when I tossed the message-strewn paper in the flames and watched them turn to ash, but Andra had been secretive herself, and it bolstered my original intention to keep our discussions private. If only Master Codiff hadn't interrupted us, the need for even more subterfuge would be unnecessary. Because of my time in Palle's kitchens, an afternoon visit would not seem suspicious in the least.

When it was close to midafternoon, fearing I might miss my sign, I wandered down to the kitchens and began chatting with Palle, discussing upcoming dinners and laughing at her slightly cantankerous wit and care. I sat at a stool close to the outside doors and gingerly ate an apple as we talked. Soon enough, footsteps sounded on the outdoor stairs, and a light rapping against the stone frame signaled Milly's entrance, who stood hesitantly at the entrance.

"Come in, child. Come in." Palle huffed when she noticed the girl. "How often must I tell you; you are free to bring deliveries into the kitchen as needed."

Milly simply nodded and scurried past, depositing a large woven basket on a counter farther in the room. "As you wish, ma'am," she replied, turning to bob a quick curtsey at me in turn.

"My lady," she muttered, her face downcast for a moment before the full weight of those dazzling golden irises rose to greet me.

"Young Milly, I am glad to see you delivering your eggs as I requested."

"Yes, Lady Ingar. Once again, thank you. For all," Milly said, her hands twisting slightly with nervous energy.

"How fare you, child?" I asked, wishing to show concern and also having it. Both were important—the outward appearance and the actual intention.

"I fare well, my Lady. Thank you for asking. However, I must return to my coop soon." She thanked Palle, who offered her an indulgent smile, curtseyed to me once again, and walked from the kitchen. She gestured my way, trying to communicate something to me I could not fully comprehend. However, I knew she likely could not linger long, so I needed to make my way out the kitchens. After a few deep breaths in and out, I rose, stretched slightly, and looked around, muttering about walking for a moment in the kitchen gardens for fresh air.

"Do not linger long, my lady," Palle called in warning. "It smells of rain, and Lord Ingar would not wish to see you drenched." A sly reminder to be about my business quickly.

I made my way out the kitchen door, stepping into the overcast afternoon light. The kitchen gardens were plentiful and utilitarian, though the color and shape and smell of freshly grown vegetables, fruits, and herbs made it feel like a more magical place. I had little time for such magic this day and needed no distraction. Head down, I walked along the wall, coming to the long, darkened archway that led from the enclosed garden out to the small service entrance on the outskirts of the bailey.

Milly's hazy form was there, waiting patiently for me. "My lady," she said again out of habit.

I had no time for pleasantries or habits and proceeded directly to the business at hand. "You have a message for me from your grandmother?"

"Yes, my lady. Gran says you may ask all the questions you desire. Meet her here, in the keep kitchen gardens, this evening after dinner."

My mind raced. Dinner was a long affair most nights, so it was likely I could feign illness and sneak away for a brief meeting. Andra entering the keep undetected was another issue entirely.

"How will she manage such a thing?" I asked with no small amount of concern. It was a fortified structure meant to hold off various forms of attack, and Andra was a seemingly frail old woman.

"If you don't mind me saying, my lady, you seem to have a way around the kitchen. Palle is a good woman. I have known her all my life. She is a friend to my grandmother."

There was no concrete plan in her words, but Milly's answer gave me enough information to mull over. It was a hard choice, however. It was one thing to have private conversations in a place where both individuals were supposed to be. Quite another to knowingly allow an un-approved guest to sneak into Ingar Keep. Was I going too far? Possibly. Did I need answers? Most definitely.

Curiosity won out. "Milly, inform your grandmother I will meet her shortly after evening mealtime."

Luckily for my endeavors and my gnawing cu-riosity, Blaine and his men were in a jolly mood for evening meal. My husband greeted me with a soft kiss and kind look before tucking me into my seat beside him and focusing on his food, his drink, and the various tales and jokes batted around by the men in attendance. I ate slowly and patiently, nodded and smiled at intervals to show interest in the occurrences around me, and even stayed for a good length of time after the servants cleared my meal. There was no sign of the night winding down quickly, so I feigned exhaustion.

I had guilt. When I told him I was too tired to remain below with him and the others, my husband showed true concern. He asked after my health, asked if I had signs of a child, and summoned guards to escort me to our chambers after I gave him many reassurances. He was not a bad husband. He cared for me in his way, it was obvious. However, something compelled me forward beyond this fact. If I loved him completely, if ours was a love match in truth, I likely would never do such a thing. I respected Blaine. I loved him in a way. But it was not enough to deter me from my course, my rendezvous with Andra and the answers I sought.

I knew I had little time. Every minute Andra dallied within Ingar Keep, the likelihood of being spied on in our conversation increased. I bundled myself in my darkest cloak. Having no time to change into less conspicuous clothing, it was the best I could do. I did not light my way through the hallways but relied on muscle memory as best I could. I bumped and skidded several times, eventually making my way quietly and, hopefully, unseen to the kitchen as all those in the Great Hall thought me at rest in my bedchamber.

There, I froze. Palle stood at the work counter long after she normally left for the evening. Instead of resting in her rooms, she was in her apron, kneading dough. No one else was about. Milly had said Palle could be trusted in this, yet I hesitated until she called out to me without turning around. "I decided to make the weekly bread early. Pay me no mind. I knead and proof. Wait for a rise. Should be one to two hours." She looked at me briefly over her shoulder for a breath of time before turning back to the sticky, pliant mixture she pounded against the wood. "I expect more company long before then, especially if any hear sounds from the kitchen. Hope for time to chat with my lady before that though."

It was hint enough to confirm my own estimation of time and need. I offered no reply, only slid through the room as she pounded and scraped. The door remained wide during the day but barred at dusk, and I used the noise she made to ease it open. The darkness of night greeted me, something I saw little of outside window views. It felt strange, wrong in some way, to creep about under the cover of night, the familiar gardens and walls seeped in blacks and grays and navies so they appeared foreign.

The one thing decidedly out of place was the soft glow of a low-slung lantern in the corner of the garden, off by the twisting vines of winter squash. Andra clutched the iron ring of the lantern in one hand and held her dark cloak closed with another, waiting patiently as she stared in my direction. I hurried over, throwing glances all around as I moved with speed and silence through the meticulously kept rows of herbs and vegetables. My body was tense, expectant—not only primed for the possibility of detection but for the push for answers, more understanding, and someone to discuss the fear and suspicions lurking in the back of my mind.

When I reached the woman, she offered a nod and a tight-lipped smile but no curtsey or formal greeting. She motioned for me to follow her. We walked, silent, for several yards before coming to a crudely carved wooden bench, weathered with age and exposure to the garden elements, positioned between a row of mid-sized fruit trees and the garden wall. It offered a small area of privacy in the open courtyard. Sitting herself down slowly, Andra took a moment to let out a puff of breath and steady herself in her seat, before she began simply. "Ask your questions."

How she knew I wished to ask her things, I could not say, and her direct response caused me a slight moment of hesitation. I did not fully know how to broach the subjects. The ideas forming in my mind were odd and fantastical and might be disturbing to some. Though I could trust this woman, felt she could give me answers to new, burning questions, it was not always safe for a woman to ask things of others, reveal ideas or thoughts.

She gave me time to find my tongue. She did not push or prod. After long beats, I began, albeit haltingly. "Our first conversation, it hit on a topic I knew little about."

She let the sentence linger for a moment before turning her sharp golden eyes my way and asking, "Did you not? I find that surprising."

"How so?"

"You are a lady, raised to be a lady. With such an upbringing, a certain amount of worldly knowledge may be lacking. You lot often remain sheltered from the harsher lessons of this world. However, you were the daughter of Lord and Lady Kesser."

"Why should that matter?" I asked, pushing us closer to my point even without voicing my true questions.

"You are your mother's daughter."

"You knew my mother?"

She shook her head, then gave a sad sigh. "Knew of her, yes. I did not know her personally. What I knew, I respected and admired. I rejoiced when Lord Ingar announced your engagement. I thought it foretold of great things. Many changes."

"Do you believe in such things? Omens and foretellings?" I rushed out my words on a harsh breath.

Serious and solemn, Andra said, "Yes."

I breathed my own sigh then. "I believe my mother did as well. Maybe she even had her own gifts. She talked of dreams often with me. And my dreams... They feel so real. So full of potential in some form."

The old woman nodded in encouragement, giving me space to continue.

"I—I dream often of things that happened, sometimes, oddly enough, of things that will happen, though in a way I often find incomprehensible in the present." I swallowed, hesitating a moment before throwing away caution and relying on what I knew and felt from Andra to guide me true. I gave her my dream. "The other night I dreamed of dragons. Of you. Of Lord Ingar and the mage and eyes and fire. The you in my dreams urged me to remember, and once I awoke, I did. I found a memory I'd long forgotten, a quick harsh moment in my childhood when my mother was uncharacteristically angry with my father. When she wept over the hide of a dragon."

A noticeable flinch moved Andra's body at my final reveal, and I pressed forward. "Why? Why did my mother rage at my father over a dragon hide? A trophy he acquired from someone else, not even one he made in a hunt."

"Obviously your mother did not condone the hunting and killing of dragons," she answered softly.

"No. That may be, but it does not answer why. Why she cared then but never cared in any other hunt. Why dragons?"

"You saw a dragon kill recently yourself, Lady Ingar. Did it not leave you feeling strange and uncomfortable?"

Angered at the circling questions, I gripped the weathered edges of the bench seat in frustration. "Of course it did. Those lavender eyes. The skin that shifted and changed. But this is not what I ask of you. Why must I remember?"

"The memory of your life is not enough," she answered cryptically. "You must go back further."

"Further than my own memory? What does that even mean?"

"Look not only to who you are but who your people are, what this land was at one time, before it was Ingar."

"History, both general and familial? Historical tomes are easy enough to find, to study. My father's lineage is well documented. Do I look there in the peerage texts? My mother... My mother was a commoner, an orphan elevated in rank. I know nothing of her past, and she is now dead; there is no way to find more information, no way I know of at this."

"Books are excellent resources, but not the best reference in this case."

"Then what is, Andra?"

"Dreams and meaning. Instinct and reaction. Study those."

My frustration growing and time melting, my voice grew more harsh than necessary. "Why dragons?" I hissed.

She pulled back, as if suddenly afraid of me though I wished her no harm. I only wanted answers. She warily said, "Because dragons are not the beasts of myth. Or, more aptly, are not only beasts of the myths certain lords wish you to believe."

"Then what are they?" I asked, my breath coming in heavy pants, ideas sparking and awareness tingling across my skin.

Staring at me, molten gold locked on ice blue, she said, "I think you know that already. Whether you are ready to admit as much to yourself now is another story."

"I am no coward," I said with heat.

"I do not believe you are," she said softly. "Nor are you merely a lady."

I blinked at this, visions of eyes and skin and dreams coming together, firing synopses in my mind. "Dragons... They can't be. They can't be people."

Standing now, she reached to squeeze my arm. "Not people. But not beasts. Something different. Something you yourself feel."

I stumbled back, shutting down my brain as best I could, unwilling to think through this shift in perception, in understanding of the world around me. In understanding myself and my family, possibly, if the implications Andra hinted at were to be believed.

"No. No. But Blaine. No," I said, over and over, shaking my head. Willing it out as best I could.

"Lord Ingar believes wholeheartedly what he was told. Never questioned it, which may or may not be its own kind of sin. But he is no cruel man. The mage..." She shifted slightly, looking away, then quickly moved to me, to pull me in a hug. "Lady Ingar, I risk our talks because I believe, from what I know of who and what you are, you bring hope for a new era to these lands, a step away from old superstitions and biases. Yet, certain men planned on you becoming Lady here, including Codiff. Watch yourself when he is near. Even when he is not."

Her warning registered somewhere in my mind but horror at this new knowledge of drag- ons captured my attention. "People. Oh God, their heads. In the Great Hall." I heaved a little, nausea rolling through my gut at the mounted heads on the wall. Andra stepped back quickly to give me space when I heaved out a loud, harsh breath. I bent to my knees to let the air rush in and out, trying to ground myself with breathing as my mother had taught me so long ago.

"I cannot—I do not—What do I do?" I cried out, tears now silently running down my face.

"You do what we all do. You do as you decide you must." Andra pulled me into a soft embrace. "What I know of you so far, your decision will be right and proper, for yourself and others."

Feeling the time slipping away, I became concerned for Andra's safety. "You cannot linger any longer." I blew out before sucking in a deep breath and wiping the tears from my face. "I may have been gone too long as it is. I must return to my place in the keep and you must alight."

"I understand. Remember the way to my stall, lady. You are always welcome, for any reason."

Nodding in acknowledgement, I pulled my dark robe tightly around myself like a fabric shield and gave my farewell. Rushing back toward the kitchen door, I traced steps from memory as my mind haphazardly skidded back and forth over all I had learned, all I had discovered about the world and myself.

TWELVE

WHEN I ENTERED THE kitchens, Palle was waiting beside fresh dough loaves set aside to rise. She startled at the noise I made upon entering. Seeing it was me, she offered a small grin as she stretched in her seat and shook off the sleep from her limbs.

"My lady. Are you hungry? Would you like a small repast before you head back to your rooms? Your husband and his men are still at the tables, jolly and louder by the minute."

I especially appreciated the gentle reminder and offer of information, as I did the offer to rest for a few moments before heading to my bedchamber. The rush of knowledge and implications rattling around in my head made me jittery. I knew I would sleep little. Some calming tea and something to nibble on in a warm room would do me good.

I nodded numbly and moved to sit at my stool along the same workbench. Palle rose and held her hands out to me. When I blinked at her, unsure of what she wanted, she whispered, "Your cloak, my lady. Not appropriate attire for the castle. How about a robe?"

I handed the dark cloak over, as it was clearly meant for hiding and not nightly strolls from room to kitchen for small foods. She bustled to the darkened larder and emerged with one of my ivory cotton dressing gowns she must have stored in there earlier. How she got it, I did not know.

"Thank you." I slipped on the soft garment and wrapping myself tight so no part of my dress showed save the bottom hem of my skirt, which could, in the dull light, look like any other night gown if one did not study it too closely. "I did not think," I muttered with regret heavy in my voice.

"You had other things on your mind. Other things on your mind still, aye? Come then. Have a seat and drink some flower tea. It will help warm and calm you. Have a cookie while you're at it. Sweets always help."

Palle shuffled around the kitchen, preparing the snack for me as quietly and efficiently as she could, while I sat slumped, exhausted, a mess of horrible ideas connecting together to tell a very different story of the world around me.

She set a small cup of tea in front of me, the saucer lined with dainty, flaky butter cookies. The scent of lavender hit hard, from either the tea or the sweets, and my mind reeled back to lavender eyes in a severed head. I shuddered hard, pushing the cup and dish away so forcefully, they tumbled to the floor and shattered.

"Oh, no. Palle. I do apologize. I just…" I couldn't finish. I could only choke out, "The heads. Do you know?"

Palle sucked in a breath, knowing what I asked, even if I did not fully explain. Her pained expression told their own tale as she offered a sad nod in reply. "One reason I choose to stay in my part of the keep."

"Is this common knowledge? How do you know? Why didn't I know?" I jumped up to pace, ignoring the bite of porcelain into flesh, letting out only a soft hiss in answer to the pain. My voice was rising with each question, and Palle moved quickly to quiet me, taking my shoulders in her hands and bending down into my face.

"Now is not the time nor the place to break like the delicate teacup on my kitchen floor, Lady Ingar. You are made of stronger stuff," she gritted out.

Her words were a slap to my face, enough to pull me from the spiraling trance I'd been in since leaving Andra's cottage. I met her gaze, hardened my own, and gave a curt nod while straightening my spine along with my mind. I had time to think, to figure out, to ponder. I did not have time to break, as Palle had so kindly reminded me.

She shoved me down, not hard but with enough force to make her point clear, and tut-tutted as she bent low to look at my bleeding foot. "Now look at this mess," she muttered, dabbing at the cut. When I moved to clean it myself, she shooed my hand away. "No. It is my kitchen. I look after what is here."

Patting me gently on the hand, she pulled loose the shard of broken cup and pressed my wound until the bleeding stopped. She moved to a cupboard for a clean cloth, which she tied around my foot, then gathered a broom and pan, swept up the remaining broken bits in a neat pile, and discarded them quickly before setting a cup of warm milk in front of me from a pan simmering in the hearth. It was a flurry of silent action, of astute care and concern that left me feeling warmth and gratitude long before I brought the milk to my lips. Palle harrumphed when I stared at my new glass and muttered, "Always a good idea to have backups and options," before she turned to check her bread.

"Drink up, my lady. The bread is almost ready for the fires."

I let the warm milk wash down my throat, the heat calming my nerves, freeing my mind. "Thank you," I said again. It seemed I thanked Palle often here. She did so much for me without my asking, somehow knowing what I needed before I did. It was touching and, I had to admit, slightly frustrating.

"Bah. Think nothing of it, my lady," she said on the wave of a hand, taking a seat across the bench from me. She brought up the weather, the baking of bread, and the warmth of the kitchen—several small topics to lead us, and likely my mind, out of the heavy questions for the time being.

Then we both heard it, the deep and intentionally intrusive clearing of a throat at the threshold to the hallway. I saw Palle's face harden and knew who I would find when I made a quarter turn on my stool to glance behind me. Master Codiff stood there, rigid, scrutinizing Palle, then piercing me with a stare.

"Lady Roselle, I thought you too tired for company," he said on a sneer, looking me up and down.

"I am tired, yet not sleepy. I thought warm milk may help."

"Would you like a draught?" he asked, a little too eager for my liking.

"No, thank you. Unnecessary. The milk will suffice. I am just now about to head again to my rooms."

"You should do that, my lady. It appears you injured yourself somehow." Codiff sniffed, pointing at the blood I only then noticed speckled the hem of my dress and the makeshift bandage wrapped around my foot.

"'Tis nothing," I said hastily.

Palle interjected. "I broke a cup earlier, Master Codiff. Poor dear found a sliver of glass I missed." She gestured at the pile of shards on top of the refuse.

He huffed, then stated baldly, "Ensure you discuss the matter with the head housekeeper. Such mishaps, especially those that harm our lady, should not go unanswered."

Palle gave a half laugh of disgust and ignored the mage, a response I noticed spike hate in Codiff's stare. Weary and protective, I replied, "There is no need to discuss the incident further, with any other person. I am fine." I finally thought to ask, "What brings you to the kitchens this late, Master Codiff?"

He bristled at my questioning and replied, "I heard voices."

"Only us womenfolk here," I said, a bitter smile on my lips. "Now, I must be to bed. Palle, thank you again for all you have done this evening. Codiff, if you'll excuse me?"

I bundled up to leave, and the mage stopped me with a firm hand to my wrist as I attempted to pass him. "Oh, no, my lady. I cannot leave you injured and alone, roaming the halls at such an hour. I shall escort you to your bed-chamber."

I nodded curtly and he turned, looping his arm in mine. It would be a gentlemanly manner from anyone, yet his touch made my skin crawl, and his grip felt forceful and too tight. It was a form of control he wielded, not aid. I blocked it out as best I could, as well as his recriminations of how I, yet again in his mind, was being too familiar with women whom I should not concern myself with and whom I should set myself above. I simmered as he lectured all the way back to my chambers. I was thankful to leave him outside, even if he gave a grave grin and promised to once again acquaint my husband with my actions. I wondered, leaning against the sturdy oak door after shutting it in his face, if Codiff knew more of my actions than he had let on. If he knew more of what I discovered that evening.

Thirteen

My eyes were tired from a sleepless night. Blaine had come in late, stumbling. I feigned sleep to avoid interacting with him as he burrowed into our bed and threw his arms around me with a contented sigh. Part of me felt bad about my actions—not only pretending to be asleep but also not immediately discussing my concerns explicitly with him in the past or the horrors I had discovered that evening. Not all of me felt bad, however. Some of me resented him, the freedom he had to do and say and represent his ideas and questions to anyone and everyone without hesitancy or fear. His certainty in this world and its rightness, which Andra herself had pointed to that night. His apparently blissful ignorance, possibly even willful ignorance. Who knew for sure? I had much to ponder, and I did so late into the night while he snored beside me, sleeping soundly.

The next day, he rose early and gave me a rough kiss, scratching my face slightly with his beard as he did. His voice, like most mornings, was low and rumbly and tugged at something in my gut when he said, "I would have you for breakfast, wife, but I must away." He left without further word, was not even present when I arrived downstairs to eat twenty minutes later. Codiff sat rigid and staring, so I grabbed a corner of bread and a small chunk of cheese and exited without delay, deciding a day spent in my workroom would be far more favorable.

It was, despite my exhaustion. The rich colors jumped from the gray rock background of the mountains surrounding Ingar. After what I had learned, the mountains seemed to tower, loom even. The tapestry used it as backdrop for other, more vibrant things: tufts of sheep, colored market stalls, blazing sun and azure sky, armored men in metallic threads, and waving banners in a riot of colors. It was Ingar in miniature. Not a point-by-point likeness but rather the spirit of the place, of the things I had seen and known and cared for while in these lands. Blaine stood central in it all, a benevolent Lord Ingar around which everything flowed, and I was happy to think of him in this way. Even if new knowledge crept and made such feelings uncertain for a time.

Like many artists, my focus was precise. I paid little attention to what happened around me as I worked, weaving thread, changing color, and mapping my next stitch. That was, until I heard "Palle" whispered in a shocked tone. Thinking I'd find my friend made a surprise visit out of the kitchens for some reason, I looked up from my work with a smile. She was not there. Only three ladies-in-waiting were in attendance, grouped in a corner and whispering.

Knowing one of them must have spoken her name, I pretended to go back to my work while listening closely. It was only when I heard the word "dismissed" hissed that I let go of my pretense and faced the ladies fully.

"What did you say?" I asked, dropping the thread and weaving in the needle I held as I turned sharply on the trio.

"Nothing, my lady," one of the women, Maria, said demurely.

I was in no mood for pretense or subterfuge. Suddenly worried for the kind woman I liked a great deal, I pushed. "No. You were discussing Palle of the kitchens. I heard as much. Tell me what you said." Remembering myself more, I did add "please, Lady Maria."

Maria blinked and studied me for some time. We were not friends, as I was not friends with any of the ladies-in-waiting. I did not outright dislike them, and I did not think they disliked me as such, but all were loyal to Lord Ingar, knew him from a young age if not their entire lives, and I was new. Someone to respect because of connection and position, though not someone to confide in. Given time and proximity, that might change. However, expectation, history, loyalty, codes of conduct, social niceties, and judgments—these factors, and many more, piled high, created a barrier between us. I knew this, resented it, and on some level resented these women. As they likely resented me in turn. It was a game we were raised to play, and players may shift and change, may grow or cast aside allegiances given certain situations.

Making her own play, Maria did not feign ignorance or offer pushback. She squared her shoulders, then stated, "Palle was dismissed from her post this morning."

"On whose authority?" I asked through gritted teeth, my tone sharp with outrage.

"Master Codiff," she replied with a bold stare in my direction.

I did not take my leave of the ladies in the workroom. I did not pack away my tapestry carefully as I usually did. Instead, I stormed out, the heat of anger propelling me quickly upward toward Codiff's study chambers in the high east tower of the keep.

It took time to reach the highest tier of the east tower, where Codiff studied and dwelled. I knew this to be intentional. More than once I had overheard him speaking on the fact that his experiments and studies were delicate or that he did not wish to be disturbed when in the middle of his important work.

Sadly for him, my anger did not dissipate during my trek up those long, winding stairs. It grew with each slamming step on stone. He had no right to any more privacy and seclusion than any other member of the keep. He especially had no right to the running of the keep, which was firmly within my domain as lady. Cooks fell within those confines. And it was Palle, my friend, who had suffered his misplaced wrath and inflated sense of authority. By the time I reached his iron-studded door, I was breathing heavily from my exertion and my stoked rage. I took a second to compose myself, hold and control my breath, and knocked firmly.

He took long, so long in fact I was about to knock again, and louder, when he finally flung the door open. His scowl showed clear annoyance, likely from being disturbed, but it quickly gave way to shock at seeing me at his threshold. "My lady," he said on a slight bow. "Whatever are you doing here? Surely the effort—"

I cut off his words with a raised hand and a haughty look, one every lady knows well. "My effort is none of your concern, Master Codiff. I come on keep business, business in which you have meddled without leave or right."

He countered. "If this concerns the cook I dismissed this morning, I assure you I had both right and reason."

Calmly, much more calmly than I felt with the boiling anger still churning in my gut, I stated, "Explain your reason."

Codiff balked at this. "I see no need to expla in..."

I moved into his space swiftly, swiftly enough that the mage shuffled back and stumbled a step. Before he recovered, I pressed my advantage. "Am I not Lady Ingar?"

He nodded and opened his mouth to reply, but I continued, ignoring his hiss of exasperation.

"As Lady Ingar, am I not tasked with the care and maintenance of this keep?"

"Yes, my lady."

"As Lady Ingar, am I not the person in charge of kitchen issues, housekeeping, grocer tallies, and menu planning?"

"Yes, but—"

I stepped farther into his space, close enough I was required to tilt my head up to stare daggers at him. "And as Lady Roselle of Ingar, am I not an authority in this land, an authority matched solely by my husband, Lord Blaine Ingar?"

Codiff hissed a reply. "Such an assertion is debatable." He gathered himself, likely remembering who he thought he was in these lands, and I saw that assurance and confidence fill him. He loomed, growing slightly taller so as to tower over me more, intimidate me with size and the crowding of his body.

I, however, did not back down but met his gaze, held my ground, and stared hard, my hot eyes back at him. "You hold no authority in this keep not given by Lord Ingar."

"The same could be said of you, my lady. Yet I have official position and place within the keep. Have held the place and position for many years. Long before your arrival. Long before your husband became Lord Ingar, in fact."

"Is Lady Ingar not an official position?" I asked, cocking my head.

"It is. It is also nebulous, in terms of authority."

We stared unblinking, neither backing down, for long moments. I felt my anger at the world, the awful truth plastered on the walls of the Great Hall, and this horrid man's disrespect. It rose in me, filled me to the brim, a living, breathing thing moving and stretching for room beneath my skin. My breath became heavy, my eyes hard and hot, feeling itchy and overly warm as if coming down from a fever. Codiff's gaze on mine turned to a question he did not voice. He blinked in confusion, and his hand shot out to grab me by the back of the neck and bring my face even closer to his own. There was a hint of fascination and strain in his breath. "Your eyes."

I tore myself away, scalded by his touch, a touch I had only experienced in intimacy, with people I loved and cared for in the past and present. Codiff's grip on my neck was not romantic or loving. It was not sexual. It was as if I were a thing to study, something he could take or control at his will without thought or consequence. It made my anger double.

"You do not touch me," I hissed.

Codiff blinked, looking down at his hand as if realizing his mistake in the moment. "My lady, I apologize."

His attempt to smooth over the incident did not hide his shrewd gleam or his air of entitlement that seemed impenetrable. I pulled straight, stepped into the hallway, and turned my back to him without another word, a snub sure to burn a man such as him. I stopped two steps down and did not look back when I gave a proclamation. "I will hire Palle back. I will also have words with Lord Ingar. Then we shall see about our places and positions."

FOURTEEN

I DID NOT RETURN to my tapestry. A sad fact, as I had neglected my work for some days previously. After the conversation with Codiff, I knew I could not concentrate on the delicate weaving. I went in search of Blaine, wandering various spots in the keep for the remainder of the morning with no sign of my husband. I eventually found his butler, who informed me Lord Ingar was out surveying distant pastures and would not return until late in the night.

There were two reasons this information was more than slightly annoying. One, I wished to speak with him about Palle and Codiff immediately, and to me, it seemed an urgent matter requiring his attention. Two, he had not informed me of his plans himself. When he had kissed me good-bye in the morning, he had told me nothing of what he would do with his day. I realized he rarely told me much of what he did with his days. Oftentimes, when I needed him, I searched the keep unsuccessful-ly, forced to wait to discuss whatever I required much later in the evening.

My scalding anger at Codiff's actions and words simmered beneath the surface. Coupled with my growing annoyance at Blaine and the realization of how his days operated without my understanding or his consideration, I determined time spent learning more about dragons was necessary. In fact, a day locked away in Blaine's study was required.

I eased into the room and took my time browsing the shelves of books, plucking out the occasional history tome that caught my attention. When I reached the far corner of the room, I noticed for the first time a section of low shelving hidden by the bulk of Blaine's massive desk. Something of seeming interest was tucked away in the corner behind a set of locked cabinet doors. The wicker fronts allowed a small view of the interior, showing shadows of books neatly stacked and organized. These were secret and safe for some reason, and my growing curiosity with my life and the world around me, coupled with my anger at the men in the keep, pushed me forward.

I tested the lock. It was sturdy, holding fast and true. Though there was one stroke of luck. Flimsy wicker weaving connected the mechanism holding the lock to the door panel. A weaving I could easily unravel and rework given my experience. I carefully unspooled the tiny strips of reeds made malleable like thick thread, winding it in on itself and tucking it into the tiny holes of the screens to return at a future date. It took patience and long minutes, but it was no matter. I was sure no one would disturb me. After a time, the bolt housing wobbled, then broke free from the frame, swinging uselessly at an angle.

The books inside were weathered with use and age, though the layer of dust proved no one had disturbed for a long time. No surprise, that. My husband was not an avid reader. A number looked like journals from past Lord Ingars, tall leather-bound volumes preserved for legacy and remembrance. The label on the newest looking book read "Lord Baxter Ingar"–Blaine's father. I remembered the previous Lord Ingar only a little. He was at best a hazy memory in the back of my mind, a large man who looked a little like Blaine but with a stony face and rigid stance. He had visited my father periodically in my childhood.

I slid the volume from its home and rubbed the supple, tanned leather in my hands, tracing the engraved name and title on the front cover. It was a thing of beauty, and my hope was it would also be a thing of knowledge, shedding light on the questions about my own history, Blaine, Ingar, and possibly dragons.

After tucking it between two large historical texts I had plucked from the open shelving, I took time to weave, winding the delicate wicker back in place so the lock at least appeared secure and in its original position. Happy with my work, I rose and pulled the three books close to my chest. I thought it best to start there. I determined there was no need to overthink my research at the beginning. History and diary would give me more information, and possibly lead me in new directions for future study.

I soon discovered Lord Baxter Ingar was pompous, callous, and calculated. The diary began like many others. It was a month-to-month rendering of events in slanted, bold script, starting when the previous Lord Ingar had taken over upon his father's death. Most entries were no more than a few clipped sentences. Some were longer, yet none reached over three paragraphs in length.

I started to turn through pages at a rapid pace, looking for larger chunks of text and skimming over the shorter, less detailed entries. They would give me no solid information beyond the mundane workings of Ingar Keep, which I was becoming familiar with through my own experience. Eventually, I gleaned small tidbits of information on the subject of dragons.

The previous Lord Ingar referred to them early in the diary. He talked of the caves along the Ingar mountains, much as Blaine had. Seems that was traditionally where dragons nested. He talked of decapitation, which was gruesome but no real surprise, given the way Blaine introduced me to dragon hunting. Baxter Ingar had also hunted, early and often it seemed. He relished in the blood and thrill. His dragon-slaying entries were always much more detailed than the others.

About four years into the diary, I found a cryptic dragon entry: "I studied my kill, watched it turn into a beast, from skin to hide and wings. Could've killed it before, strong but not as strong then, but no. Much less skill required for easier prey." The idea of transformation was key. A flitting between. Could they turn, to and fro, from person to dragon? Was this widely known? How had I never known? I suspected much in myself, my past, and every piece fell into place, forming a more disturbing picture. There was much more to discover here about the creatures who haunted my dreams and now, my memory. I needed to know more yet had no one to safely turn to for answers.

Reaching into Ingar's past gave glimmers of knowledge but also produced more questions.

Shutting the book with a huff of annoyance, I stopped my research for a quick respite. I shoved the diary, along with the histories, in my cedar chest. Blaine would not look there, as he had no interest in the trinkets of remembrance I kept within. Determined to return to it later, I prepared for bed, stoking the dying fire myself before crawling into the sheets and lying awake for far too long, waiting for sleep to take me.

When he returned late in the night, long after I spent more time reading his father's book, Blaine muttered words. Caressed and kissed me in a bid for my attentions. I feigned sleep and ignored his desire. He eventually gave up with a sigh, gently kissed the top of my head good night, and curled into me to sleep himself. He was fast asleep within moments, like a babe unburdened with worry or doubt.

Once again, it took time for me to drift into a fitful rest, and when I finally slept, the dreams came again. Fire. Death. Blood. My mother's cry. My own eyes sparked, a clear reflection I saw in the wicked gleam of Codiff's stare. The silent urging of Andra. The diary opened and shining in the darkness. I awoke overheated, drenched with sweat and a pant on my tongue. I stared in the darkness for several beats, willing my heart to slow and thinking on the glowing diary, an addition to the dreams. I lay back, pulled the cover around myself despite my sweat, and turned into Blaine, flinging an arm and leg around his large, solid body. It was a tangible thing I could touch and ground myself in for the moment. He stirred, grumbled in sleep, and turned away from me so that I hugged him from behind, wide awake as he slept on.

Fifteen

Admittedly, I slept late the next morning. The night before had been restless, and Blaine's morning greetings barely penetrated my sleepy mind. The sun shone bright, creeping midway to its pinnacle, by the time I rolled myself out of the bed and prepared for my day. I did hurry once I remembered my task for that day: discuss Codiff's behavior with Blaine, then find and reinstate Palle.

I skipped a late-morning meal, avoiding the sadness I would feel entering the keep kitchen and not finding Palle commanding the others and fussing over my need for nourishment. I hurried to my husband's study, hoping he was there and I would have no need to waste time searching for him around the grounds.

I heard his soft boom as I drew closer and let out a sigh of relief, only to have it catch in my throat when I recognized the sinister, nasal tone of Codiff also coming from the study. The door was slightly ajar, so I stood motionless, straining to hear what the men said.

"Whatever do you mean?" Blaine asked, confusion and a hint of dismissiveness in his voice.

"Sire. Lord Ingar. I know it may be hard to fathom. However, there were very particular reasons your father wished you to marry Lady Roselle. Reasons he was never able to fully explain before his untimely death at the claws of those vile creatures. He was a student and a hunter, your father. We talked long about what could be, and Lady Roselle was important to such plans. Her bloodline is important."

"Yes. Yes. She comes from a long line of nobles. All ladies in this age do."

"No, my lord. I do not speak of her father, but of her mother. Do you remember Lady Corine?"

"Of course, though I did not see her often. She always appeared poised, lady-like despite her upbringing. Had such kind eyes. The same eyes as my lady wife, if I recall correctly."

"Exactly. Those eyes. Yesterday..."

Codiff stopped abruptly when a passing chambermaid I had not noticed behind me stopped to bow and loudly greet me by title. I returned the niceties but saw Codiff and my husband silently standing at the opened doorway when I turned back to hear more.

"Husband. Good day," I replied to their looks, ignoring Codiff completely as both bowed slightly and stepped aside to allow me entrance into the room.

"Lady wife," Blaine muttered, reaching for my hand and placing a soft kiss on the back. When he looked up from it, I saw worry. Maybe a little curiosity as well, but worry dominated. "Are you well? You slept deep this morning."

"Yes. I am well. Thank you." Turning to finally acknowledge Codiff with a curt nod, I continued. "I am glad to see Mage Codiff in attendance, as I had an issue I wished to discuss with you that concerned his actions yesterday."

"Codiff has explained, Roselle. No need for you to worry. The careless cook is gone now, and you can concern yourself with finding a new, more suitable replacement."

"But the point, husband, is Palle was not careless. Far from it. She was an excellent head of the kitchen."

"Codiff informed me she allowed you to be hurt in her kitchens. Something about broken dishes and your delicate feet."

"That was nothing, Blaine."

Codiff slid into the conversation. "I beg to differ, my lady. I had your utmost concern in mind when I dismissed the former cook."

Countering Codiff's claims, I vehemently attempted to assure Blaine. "The cut was nothing, my lord. A small thing of my own doing."

"Did she not also allow that woman, Milly, to frequent the kitchens?" he pressed, standing straighter, his face pinched and his arms crossing his chest.

"Completely my doing, husband. I hired Milly to deliver eggs to the kitchens."

"We discussed that woman—"

"That girl, Milly, does no harm and only comes to the kitchens through the service entrance," I said in a clipped voice, annoyed by the direction of the conversation and his refusal to listen to me.

Blaine, grating at my tone and the blatant interruption, gritted out, "A proper cooking woman would allow none such as her entry into her kitchens. Once again, I must remind you of your position as it relates to this Milly. She should be far from you, far from this keep."

Finding the anger rising in me, I stared Blaine down, defiant and unmoving in the face of his annoyance. "My position is the exact thing in question here. The exact issue I have with Codiff's actions. As lady of this keep, am I not in charge of the employees, especially those in the kitchens?"

"Traditionally, yes. However, if I cannot trust you to run my home properly..." He let the sentence fall, and I fumed as the silence between us lasted long beats.

"Prior to the mage coming to speak with you on such topics that should be of no concern to him, did you have issue with my running of the keep?" I hissed.

"I was unaware of your dealings, as I seem to be unaware of much concerning my young wife," he countered, not budging in his rigid posture. He did search my face for something, likely whatever Codiff saw there yesterday.

"Am I to lose my position in this keep? In relation to the servants and staff? In relation to you?" I yelled, unable to control my anger and my hurt at what he was saying and implying. I may have been coming to similar realizations about our relationship, but I wished to mend those breaks. Blaine targeted them in his anger at me.

"If you cannot act as a proper Lady Ingar should!" he boomed back, looming over me as he did, heated breaths rushing in and out of his half-opened mouth.

I gasped, shocked he uttered such a threat aloud—his willingness to forsake me—even if he said it in the heat of a momentary anger. I blinked away the tears that started pooling and

I looked down quickly, hoping he did not see them.

Of course he did. He sighed sadly and said, "Leave us."

I heard Codiff shuffle from the room and close the door behind him, but I was too busy not looking at Blaine. With my back toward him, facing his desk, I thought of the locked panel I knew was there and tried to focus on what I could learn, what questions I had, and what I needed to know. Anything to help ease the sting of those words from a man I was trying so hard to love.

"Little Light," he whispered, coming up behind me to wrap his arms around my midriff.

I stood straight and unyielding, giving him nothing, letting only silence linger.

"I was angry because you do not do what you should," he confessed.

I offered nothing in return.

"Come now, Little Light. My wife. My Roselle. You are mine as I am yours. You know this." He kissed the top of my head, leaning his cheek there after. "I only wish to help you do better. I never want to hurt you."

I turned, still stinging from the words but needing more from him in order to move forward. "I must feel safe to be who I am here.

Valued. Trusted. Your words do not help this effort."

"A marriage spat, that is all," Blaine said dismissively, hugging me tightly to himself. "One of many we will have in our long life together, dear wife."

"What of Codiff?"

"You should respect Master Codiff, but I will have words with him regarding the difference between his duties and your duties."

"And Palle?"

"Let us not go back to that topic just yet," he said with a sigh and a tight squeeze of my body. "I will heed your council on such in future, but for now, let us leave this particular fight be."

I nodded against his strong chest, burrowing in without a sound. I wanted that safety. That protection. I wanted to be a part of Ingar—the land and the man—in a way I could know, deep in my bones, I would have security, peace, and influence. None of that was certain, especially if I did not push for my place now. But for a moment, tired and unsure in all things and raw from new ideas and lingering doubts, I wished more than anything this were already true, that I had no need to fight and claw my way toward it. Wished I already had a place in the heart of this man who may be complacent and may be dismissive but seemed to care to some degree.

How far such care extended, how long it would last if he learned harder truths, was like the issue of Palle—a fight for another time.

Sixteen

Palle weighed heavy on my mind. I hoped she was well, and I planned to reinstate her position soon. There was no way to get word to her, no way I could trust, aside from Andra. The night market, a monthly occurrence, was fast approaching. It was one of the few times Blaine himself went to the market, and I knew I could get away from the rabble around my husband long enough to speak with Andra. She would deliver my message to Palle and answer a few more questions as needed. My questions were piling up, higher and higher, a practical hoard I wished to trade for more knowledge, more certainty.

In the days between, I spent time completing my tapestry. Glimmering threads added texture and luster to the overall piece in a pleasing way. It shimmered in spots, shine peeking through here and there against the more mundane materials to offer a bit of interest, a moment of mystery and delight. The whole was impressive. Measuring close to my height in both length and width, it was a large and intricately designed piece. Blaine was still a focal point, as was the keep. I placed myself there, a straight and stoic figure at the door to the Ingar stronghold, protecting it as Lord Ingar, in my depiction, appeared to protect the land and its inhabitants. Animals and people milled around in sections of street and field and wood, all ringed by rugged mountains on the outskirts—mountains where small caves lay hidden. The outer edge had a floral border, a blue, purple, and pink mixture of the lupine and fireweed that grew naturally in the hills and valleys of those surrounding mountains. A day or two more and I would be done. The tapestry would hang in the Great Hall for all to see, a sign of my care and concern for this place and these people.

Whenever I had moments alone in our chambers, I also continued to read. The histories were dry and predictable, outlining the same lessons I had learned as a young woman with the tutors hired by my guardian. The familiar story, their banishment from the realms of men and the subsequent long and bloody fight against them throughout the years, was told from the same perspective: dragons condemned as dangerous and unpredictable creatures. All of it now read as biased, slanted. That was the way with histories most often. Written by victors, it colored the world in a particular light based on the victory, the fighters, and the ones deemed the enemy. I learned little I did not already know, except the claim that Ingar lands was the original start of the dragon wars, the place where dragons were first driven out from society. Whether this was truth or exaggeration based on another type of bias, I could not say. As I was collecting all the information I could, I filed it away with the other ideas to be mulled over later.

Lord Baxter's diary was more interesting. Most entries were minimal, though they showed the general outline and attitude of a rigid, harsh, and domineering man. Getting to know my long dead father-in-law made me thankful he was not a part of my life, though the guilt of such thoughts tugged at me. When Blaine spoke of his father, though it was a rarity, he described the man with reverence and respect. I wished the diary allowed me to see the son's perspective, as all I saw led to dislike and mistrust.

Eventually, a pattern emerged through my skimming. Dragons, and the hunt for dragons, appeared more frequently every six months or so. There were times in winter and summer when he discovered a dragon lurking through some means and dispatched it. However, the hunting parties occurred in spring and fall, the rising and waning seasons. In these times, there were dragon hunts discussed every month, sometimes a few referenced at once. It matched what I knew from my limited experience: Blaine did not go hunting for his dragon until the frost left Ingar and spring rain tinged the air. I wondered if he had plans to hunt again soon, if indeed this time of year was dragon-hunting season.

On the day preceding the night market, I spent the afternoon alone in our chambers. The ladies-in-waiting and my husband expected me to rest in order to engage in the market later that evening. I read instead, digging into what was the twentieth year of Lord Baxter's monthly diary. I was hoping to see more of Blaine in these pages, but the father spent no time discussing his son beyond the fact that he had an heir and would train him in all the Ingar ways. In the early spring of that year, there was a longer entry, one connected directly to what I sought, though I was not happy to read it.

"Dragon killed, her head taken, her blue eyes so familiar I immediately recognized them. Took her hide, laden with jewels. Invited Lord

Kesser to a meet and gifted him the pelt on his own lands. Show that creature I know what she is. Hope she choked on her tears for her vanquished kin."

I blinked, reread. I suspected all this, though I did not know. I had hinted at it to Andra, and she to me, but it was not uttered. Here it was, meshing with my memories, the quiet part whispered aloud. My mother was kin to dragons. I was somehow part dragon. And Lord Baxter had known this all along, revealed in cruelly asserting his knowledge. I slammed the book shut and tossed it away, unable to stomach its presence. I shook with fear and disgust. Why was I never told this? Did others know?

My mind went to Codiff. He knew. He hated me from the start yet wanted me as Blaine's wife. Why? How does being part dragon help Blaine, or Ingar, or Codiff? I shook again, more questions running through my mind, but a certainty also settled there, making me focus. I was part dragon. My memories and dreams told me as much. My conversations with Andra pointed toward it. Lord Baxter's private words confirmed it. My mind and heart knew it, felt it. I held heat and power in myself somehow, and dammit, I was going to find a way to use it.

Blaine entertained a jovial smithy and our entourage a few stalls away. His smile was bright, open. It made my heart lurch a bit when I wondered if Baxter had smiled when he killed my kin, if Blaine knew what I was and still killed those like me.

With my husband and our guard distracted, I took the opportunity to sneak away. I had questions that required swift answers. Andra smiled at me from her stall opening, but her golden eyes turned hard when she noticed something about my look. Pulling us both quickly into the depths of her stall, she asked, "What do you know, Lady Ingar?"

I appreciated the immediacy in her words, her own need to know, and decided direct questioning was the best way to go. "I read histories, and Lord Baxter Ingar's diaries." Andra sucked in a harsh breath at the admission, knowing exactly the man he had been and what I had likely found in those pages. Still, I needed confirmation and answers, so I pressed forward with questions of my own. "Am I a dragon?"

Andra blinked at the bold question, sighed, and answered honestly. "Part dragon. Your mother was a dragon. I know this as fact not because I knew your mother, but because I knew her sister, a woman Lord Baxter Ingar killed many years ago."

I trembled at the confirmation of my heritage, my memory, my reading of Baxter. Shaking it off as quickly as I could, I pressed on. I had little time to linger.

"What exactly does this mean? And how does it connect with Lord Baxter Ingar and Codiff?"

"In essence, power. A Lord Ingar with the magic of dragons in his veins would be a formidable lord indeed, one whose lineage connected to another lord of this land. A family going back centuries would grant such a lord legitimacy. You could make all this happen for Ingar. For the mage, a child born in his care, trained to his tutelage, would be a fount of natural magic he could access and control. Given the magic and power on offer, even with Lord Baxter Ingar and Mage Codiff's hatred of dragons, they set your betrothal."

"I have no magics. No powers to speak of. What would I pass down?"

"Dragons are both born and made, my lady. You are a person with the capability of changing, morphing into something more. You hold the potential inside yourself, but you also express it in ways you do not recognize, like your dreams. Prophetic dreams are an ability some dragons are known to possess."

I had known my dreams were special. They held knowledge. My mother raised me to believe so, even if I had forgotten for a time. The prophetic nature, baldly stated, was no real surprise. The idea of turning, of becoming, however, that was something wholly new.

"I can turn, can become a dragon?" I asked, possibilities, good and bad, crowding my mind at the mere idea.

"Aye," she replied with a serious stare. "Your magic is there. I feel it, and you speak of it when you talk of your dreams, whether you realize it or not. It only remains dormant, not inaccessible. You could activate it, with knowledge and patience and belief."

Belief. Assurance. Those were lacking at the time, buried along with the magic in my blood. "Why do it?" I whispered, more to myself, thinking of consequences and repercussions.

Andra took my hand and shook it gently in her wrinkled grip. "It is who you are, my lady. A part of you. Your legacy and your heritage." She paused, taking a deep breath before she continued. "I cannot predict your future. What transformation could bring to you personally. I can say to change, to become who you were meant to be, can help others do the same. And if enough people change, become new and different and strong, throw away old fears and biases, it can tip the scales of our world, change the course of our lives and future lives."

"Even if I want that and disregard all the ways it could go horribly wrong for me and all I hold dear, how would I even go about doing it? How is such a thing physically possible?"

"You decide to embrace who and what you are. Pull on the magics now dormant inside you. See what emerges. That is all I know, the best advice I can give."

She dropped my hand and patted my shoulder gently before turning from me as if she knew I needed a moment of semi-privacy. A few tears slipped free, shed for what I was and what I could never be and what my people must have suffered. Of what my mother must have suffered. I shook it off as quickly as I could, promising myself time and space to make a decision, think through not only what to do next, but what the entire direction of my life would be, could be, given what I now knew.

Yet there was Blaine to consider. Would he accept my change, my magic, my ability? Did he even know it possible? Could we build a better future together, for ourselves and all of Ingar, possibly all of the world of men?

Seventeen

I hurried from Andra's stall before anyone marked my absence in my husband's revelries. Keeping my distance, I wandered behind the small crowd around him in a distracted haze, something Blaine noticed. Thinking I was tired, he ordered me to bed like a child, but I had no will or reason to contradict him in the moment. I needed time alone to think, without the feeling that I must perform a particular role or duty to make others happy and comfortable.

In the silence of my bedchamber, the glow of the fire casting flickering shadows across the rough stone walls, I sat trying to warm myself, parse my thoughts, and connect with my own feelings. It was a novel approach, thinking of myself and what I needed or could do rather than what others needed from me or expected me to do. A vast difference in perspective, a shift in tone and understanding of life I did not fully appreciate at the time. Yet, there I sat, curled into the large chair by the blazing fire, thinking as hard as I ever had about issues of grave consequence to me, to Blaine, and to the people of Ingar.

After much time passed, I formulated the sketch of a plan. Blaine was key. He was my husband, and as such, had a right to know certain things about me were true. It was not right his father and Codiff conspired to use me as a pawn, but Blaine was also a piece in their game. If he had not realized this, he deserved to make his own choices with all the information available to him. What this might mean for me, who I was, and my position in the keep as Lady Ingar, I could not guess. It left me vulnerable. I could be homeless and penniless out on the streets. Or, worse, dead at the hands of a man I was supposed to love and who was supposed to love me. He deserved to know, yes, but I had an obligation to myself, to keep myself safe. I knew I had to proceed with caution, could not simply blurt the truth to Blaine.

With no immediate course of action determined, at least as it pertained to my husband, I sat staring into the flames and waited. Soon enough, laughter filled the keep, and I knew Blaine had returned from the night market. He did not linger long with his men. In a few short minutes, he was easing the bedchamber door open, cautious and quiet in an effort to spare my sleep. The sight of his concern melted my heart a touch and furthered my resolve to reach out to Blaine, explain as much as I knew, when I felt he was prepared for the truth.

He flashed a crooked grin my way when he saw me perched on the chair by the fire and not wrapped in bed. "Oh. Wife. I thought you would be asleep."

"Nay. I waited for you, Blaine."

"Ah. You did, did you?" he asked, his grin turning to a smirk, his eyes taking on a familiar heat. "Why would that be, Little Light?" He crossed the room on swift, sure feet, towering over me in a blink. His face softened as it looked down at me, and he brought his hand up to rub my cheek.

I turned into it, like an animal brushing against a petting hand.

"Come," he commanded, taking my hand in his and leading me toward our large bed. I followed, again not minding the command when I wished to follow it, but I stopped him short. We stood staring at each other in the dim light, me studying his face with intention, wondering, always wondering, what I could say and when.

"Roselle?" he asked at my halting.

In that moment, I had to know at least one thing before I could take another step toward our bed. "Why do you hate dragons?"

Blaine visibly started at the question, confused by the odd jump in conversation. "Dragons? Why do you speak of dragons?"

"Please, Blaine. I just... Why do you hate dragons?"

"All men hate dragons, Roselle. I no more than any other. They are vile, destructive beasts."

"Have you seen this yourself? Seen them destroy and ravage like the tales tell us?"

"There is enough evidence, scarred castle walls and cities turned to ash, to know it to be true."

"But you've never witnessed it yourself? Never seen a dragon in the process of destroying anything?"

"We hunt to avoid such," he replied, more firm, surer, pulling himself into a tall, stately posture. "As you know, my father died on such a hunt."

"Yes. Yes. True," I muttered. It would be unfair to point out to a son his father hunted for sport and was killed by the thing he hunted, which felt like consequences more than anything else. "What if? What if dragons weren't actually mindless or destructive, and we just needed to work to understand them and their magic? Would you wish to know more, be more open to them?"

He threw his arms around me, engulfing me in a strong, deep hug. "Oh, Little Light. So sweet and so naïve. So caring, you would extend your care to creatures of death." He pulled back and looked deep into my face. "I cannot fault you for such sweetness. It will serve our people and our children well. Yet, Roselle, some things do not deserve our care or thought. A wise person knows when and where to extend their mercy. Trust me when I say dragons deserve none."

I stared into his kind brown eyes and could see clearly he believed this. Believed both to the bottom of who he was—that mercy and understanding were commendable and that dragons had no right to either. In a flash, I knew what he would do if I blurted what I was to him, revealed to him my dragon nature. He would recoil. He would react harshly. In time, however, he might not. He might be more lenient, more understanding, more apt to consider rather than react based on tales he had been told since childhood. He was a good man—it clearly showed in all his actions—and his goodness could prevail. I knew it could, with patience and gentle nudgings. Which meant I did not press or push. Time is what I needed, and I was young, new to myself in many ways. I thought it might be best for us both to give the time, for Blaine to soften and me to better understand myself and my dragon nature before we confronted it together.

I truly believed we could. In that moment, I believed as Blaine believed, but it was not in the assurances of the past. Rather, I clung to the promise of a different future, one where a bias could change, old ideas confronted and slain. Blaine and I could help establish a new world, Lord and Lady Ingar working together as one. Only if I slowly worked toward change instead of demanding all at once. Remembering these thoughts, the hope and assurance they gave, I hated to admit Blaine had been right in one regard: I was naive.

My hope was real, my desire to change and be honest about who I was, to let Blaine know how history and his father had used him so ill in making him think in these ways were right. I stopped my questioning and melted against my husband. I pushed away my words and ideas and complex feelings with soft kisses that turned heated, with hands that caressed, then tugged and pulled, and with heat and sweat and fire of a different kind—the kind I associated with trusting and coming to know and love a man. I fell to the bed, Blaine a weight on top of me, and as we stroked and stoked and sought pleasure in each other, I dreamed of a world where I could be all I was in these moments and not tuck away parts of myself to make another comfortable.

Eighteen

As I so often did, I channeled my pain, uncertainty, and frustration into my art, working at a frantic pace to finish the final touches on my grand tapestry. Two days I worked, perfecting every detail, saying very little to anyone about any topic, my hands busy finishing a task while, occasionally, my mind wandered to the issues of most concern: dragons, Blaine, Codiff, and Palle.

There was one incident of note in these days. My ladies-in-waiting were present, as always, chatting softly to one another. They did not engage me in conversation, as they expected my working silences after many days together in my workroom. However, I looked up at one point, distracted from my work by the slick swish of fabrics so often marking the entrance or exit of a lady. I caught three ladies-in-waiting exiting the room, bunched together in such a way to allow whispers to pass between them. It was odd to see a group leave together when not going to a meal or arranged event, so I stared after them, wondering what I may have missed in my schedule, when a dainty cough sounded on the opposite side of the room. Turning toward the sound, I found Lady Maria staring back at me, soft hazel eyes trained in my direction.

I knew she had stayed behind and signaled her presence for a reason. What that reason was could be any number of things, good or bad, but I was not in a mood to gently discover. "Yes, Lady Maria?"

She continued to look at me, silent for several beats, before she softened. "I have news of Palle," she said, apparently also wishing to be direct.

I sucked in a breath and tears gathered. I couldn't speak for fear of them falling, and I could not let them fall, not in front of this lady, in this room where the other ladies could saunter back to spy me at any moment. I gestured with my head, a silent request for her to continue.

"Palle is the mother of my lady's maid, a woman in my service for well over a decade. Did you know this?" When I shook my head, she continued. "I've known both for years, from the keep and my own home. Fine women. Always courteous, even if a bit curt. Always helpful. Always kind." She paused, looking down at her own needle and thread, an embroidery hoop where she stitched flowers. In a hushed toned, she confided, "I may have spoken of your reaction to my maid, Ginna, who may have relayed the outcome to her mother. Ginna may have also given me word for you, from Palle, saying all is well and you are not to worry on her behalf."

My tears threatened to fall, but I steeled myself, to get out what I must. "Thank you, Lady Maria. For the information. Could you... Would you be willing to relay a message for me?"

She inclined her head in assent, and I heaved in a breath.

"Please let Palle know I will get her position back. I will." I hesitated to give more. Maria seemed genuine, a good source who could be more, but to give this wounded part of myself over to a woman who could use it against me was a risk. I decided it was a risk worth taking and said, in a soft, slightly cracked voice, "Tell her I feel lost in the kitchens now, without her order and presence."

When I looked back into Maria's face, I saw no reproach or calculation. I saw a pang of empathy, the look of a woman who found value in others, even if their rank was technically below her own. A woman who appreciated what others offered to her. A woman who would feel the same pain as I felt if those she cared for suffered. Her face, normally a soft mask, scowled for a moment. "What Codiff did, undermining your authority and firing a fine cook like Palle, is beyond the pale. I, and others, support you in this and will continue to do so." She rushed to also say, "Not all, so be vigilant. Know there are those of us who see who you are through your treatment of others, especially through your treatment of Milly and Palle, and respect you all the more for it."

Without another word, she turned back to her work, a perfect picture of a refined lady at her needle. I blinked rapidly to keep those pesky tears at bay and turned back to my weaving. I stared for long minutes, running over the brief exchange. Palle and Andra had hinted at similar ideas, but I had never expected such from a lady. It gave me even more hope for the new world I wished to create, a new era free from old biases and expectations. With women like Palle and Lady Maria on my side, I could be what Andra thought I was.

The conversation with Maria buoyed me. Palle was well, as I learned from Lady Maria, and I trusted she would know I thought of her still, missed her presence, and worked for her return. Her reinstatement was my first priority after the presentation of my tapestry. I finished the massive piece the day following my talk with Maria and had the ladies-in-waiting carefully wrap it for Blaine. I decided to give it to him that evening, in the Great Hall directly after dinner. It would be another way to connect us, another offering to ease our communication and understanding of one another. Another mark of a growing love. One, hopefully, I could also use as a basis to begin again the conversation regarding Palle, put the argument of the past behind us and start working toward the bright future we both deserved.

My dress made from Andra's fabric the color of my eyes, of cloudless blue skies in summer, was ready at the same time, and it felt like an omen of sorts. As I slipped into the dress, its rouching at the top leaving my shoulders bare, the soft lace front a delicate touch of detail, the lines of freshwater pearls down the front edges of the lace throwing an opalescent sheen, I wondered if there was more of this fabric to be had. If I could have a matching tunic commissioned for Blaine, we, the Lord and Lady Ingar, could pose as shining blue beacons against the gray mountains of Ingar. It would make a lovely portrait if ever we were to have one made.

I fidgeted with nervous excitement all through the meal, barely eating, watching my husband closely for a sure sign for when I should bestow his gift. After dinner, before he was too into his ale or his stories, there came a lull in conversation. I jumped into it, motioning for the designated ladies-in-waiting to quickly fetch the tapestry while I called for Blaine.

"My lord?"

"Yes, my lady?" he answered, a soft, indulgent smile on his lips.

"I have something for you."

"You do? Well, let's have it then, Lady Roselle." His mouth crinkled at the corners as he gave a slight chuckle. My heart flipped a bit in my chest at the masculine beauty, his attention on me, and the idea of what we could have.

With a nod from me, the servants cleared the table and the ladies-in-waiting placed the large bundle, wrapped with thin paper and twine dyed a deep crimson, directly before their lord. He tore into the package with haste and stared for a moment at the tapestry before him. As instructed, the tapestry sat folded so that the central scene, Lord Blaine Ingar among his people, faced my husband when opened. He took several beats to consider it, running his hands along the fabric and touching his own face, rendered in thread by my hand.

He laughed. A deep, hearty laugh with a tinge of indulgence. Something about the sound, his look of amusement instead of appreciation, made my heart sink. "Well done, my wife. A fine tapestry indeed. Where shall it hang?"

Staring at him for a beat, I timidly replied, "I thought here, in the Great Hall, my lord."

He turned this way and that in his large carved seat at the head of the banquet table, making a show of looking around the room. Making a joke. The company began to laugh along in small doses, his antics clearly telling everyone it was a joking matter. I found nothing funny. I had spent hours upon hours bent over this tapestry, weaving his world, with him in the center of it, and he found it amusing.

"I do not know, Little Light. It may fit best in a corridor."

More laughter ensued, and I felt the heat of shame color my cheeks. Blaine saw it and rushed to add to his assessment.

"A hallway display will allow others to get close, see your detailed work, admire up close. The Great Hall is for formal matters. Your feminine accomplishments would appear to better advantage in another part of the keep."

I stared at him in shock, not fully comprehending what he had said. I understood the words, their meanings, but what I could not understand was how he could say them, how he could dismiss my art while attempting to placate me.

Before I could gather my thoughts, hide my hurt to press for my inclusion in the Great Hall, Master Codiff jumped into the fray. He seated himself beyond my husband, on his other side, so I could not see him clearly as Blaine was still turned toward me, blocking my line of sight. However, I heard his voice, felt it creep up my spine as he said, "Very true, my lord. Very true. The Great Hall is a space for celebration and intimidation in equal measure. It needs assertive décor proclaiming the prowess of your house. Given that, I am happy to say the taxidermist finished mounting your latest kill and it is now ready to be hung here on the Ingar trophy wall."

I jolted, horror creeping in through my anger and sadness, the little food I had eaten becoming a lead weight in the pit of my stomach. Codiff clapped his hands, and two men, carrying a burlap-covered board between them, moved to place their burden before my husband. In his excitement for the presentation, Blaine snapped his fingers at a waiting servant and pointed at my tapestry. He dismissed it, utterly without thought, to have the atrocity I knew to be under the fabric placed inches from his face.

Recoiling, panic running through my veins, my head swiveled in search of an exit, escape my sole focus. I needed to do something, anything, to get away before someone pulled the fabric from the package, before I saw again what my husband had done to the dragon, to the person who had been a dragon.

As I rose slightly, I noticed Codiff's stare, a cruel smile on his face, and I knew, without doubt, he had done this on purpose, waited for a moment such as this to get the most horrific reaction from me possible. He even gave a mock bow of his head. A moment of clarity hit like a blow to my chest. The curl of his lips told me he suspected I had discovered the truth about myself. The bastard knew I knew what lay brutalized on the table, and he was playing it for some advantage.

The moment I took to look on Codiff, to process what was happening, was too long. I did not escape the Great Hall in time because as I stood, mere inches from my husband, he flung the canvas from his trophy, triumph and pride clearly written across his face, so all in the room beheld the mounted head of the dragon my husband recently killed. My mind raced, my thoughts screamed. This had been a person, a person transformed but a person, nonetheless. A person stuffed and mounted as a sign of dominance.

Worst of all were the eyes. There was no intelligent, accusatory lavender stare. Those eyes that had held so much meaning and knowledge replaced with glass, a cloudy black with no knowing or feeling present. The person who had been now turned into a mindless creature to be hung with all the others, to be pointed at when recounting the story of death and destruction in the guise of heroism. I looked into those empty black eyes where so much had been before, and my own filmed over with a haze of orange.

I felt the heat of anger fill me, and instead of calming it or burying it, I made the choice to use it. I imagined it as fire, shaped as a length of thread, one I could pull and stretch in my mind. The heat burned more intensely, filled my body until it felt like it would burst from my skin, and made my eyes water from the warmth of the blaze within.

There was a gasp from a servant, and someone farther down the table from me screamed. When Codiff and Blaine faced me, both jumped back in fear at what they saw. I didn't know what it was, how I looked, yet I knew it was enough to frighten both men, to cause the others in the room to start a rush for the door.

I reached out a hand, a hand I could see licked with soft flames, fire creeping up the sleeves of my blue dress. The flames did not burn me or my fabric but rippled like water in time to the beating heat in my blood. I tried to close the dragon's eyes, tried to give it some dignity, but the taxidermist glued them open, to forever look bleak, mindless, inhuman. I felt Blaine lurch beside me, and I turned an angry glare at him. He backed away, confusion and disgust dancing across his face in equal measure.

"Little Light?" he whispered, a note of disbelief in his tone.

"This light is not little," Codiff said, a grave look on his face.

Blaine reached out to touch me, but I hissed at him, pulling my hand away. "What are you?" he boomed after he jumped, a clear bluster to cover the physical sign of fear he had displayed.

I said nothing. No words. Looking down into the face of a person killed by this man for no other reason than their difference, I knew, in an instant, all my dreams of a future with Blaine were smoke and haze, intangible wishes that could never come true because of what we both were. I heard Codiff give a command to someone but paid no mind. My heated gaze stayed on Blaine, this man who could be so sweet to a soft and gentle lady but so cruel to something he saw as different and menacing. This man could not, would not change—this man whom I married to forever according to our laws.

I let out a scream of rage and fear and shame and lost hope that turned into a deafening roar. The sound reverberated through the Great Hall, causing the rafters to tremble and the men still standing to cover their ears in pain. I sucked in a breath, ready to give more, ready to pull on my fire and see what else I could produce, when I felt something large and heavy, swung with great force, connect with my temple. There was a bright flash of fire and pain, and the rest was darkness.

Nineteen

I awoke shivering, lying on my back on a stone floor with a pounding headache. My stomach grumbled and my mouth was smacking dry, parched. My throat ached, as did my eyes, as if I needed water to replenish after spending a hot afternoon directly under the summer sun. Once my eyes adjusted, I saw a small straw mattress in the far corner of the room. It had no bedding of any kind, only a mattress, old and stained, no more than two inches high. It would offer little comfort or cushion. As I stared at the bed, crumpled and sad next to the wall, a memory took hold, and I pulled back in horror, realizing this was the room in the tower from my dream.

A small corner window allowed light to seep into the dark room, giving me a hazy view of my surroundings. I pulled myself up for a better look, realizing how sore I was only in the moment. The pain from my head pulsed.

I touched my temple and immediately pulled my hand away at the stinging shock. It was sore and sensitive and felt knotted. I'd taken a nasty hit. Trying to tramp down the nausea caused by my waking movements, I stilled, breathing steadily in and out until the wave passed. Slowly I moved forward, toward the window, hoping I wouldn't see what I already knew to be there. Yet I did. I saw the mountains of Ingar, clear and unobstructed in the distance. I saw the bailey from a great height, the bustling people appearing small from my vantage. I was clearly in the west tower.

Turning as slowly as possible to keep from jostling my pained head overmuch, I took in the rest of my surroundings. There was a small wooden stool, a squat table with a candle stub stuck to a rusty tin holder and a tin mug of water, and the mattress. There was nothing on the walls or floor, no sign of any other object in the room, any other use for the room except to contain, to lock away. With a heavy heart and a throbbing head, I tried to heave the solid oak door, but it would not budge. A rattle hinted at a lock on the other side when I tried, again and again, to pull the door open, to get myself free.

I did not try for long, as the pain in my head threatened to make me sick once again. For a time I stared at the door, mind blank and unthinking, unable to process what was happening or what I should do next, until my thirst forced me away, toward the table and the metallic tang of the water in the old and battered tin cup. I gulped it down without forethought, feeling only momentary relief from the small amount of liquid. With nothing else to do, and pain trampling down any desire to explore, escape, or even think, I turned to the mattress and curled into a ball there, willing sleep to come.

Sleep had come, after a time, but it had offered me no dreams of guidance or assurance. It was the first dreamless sleep I remembered having in years. Outside was full dark when I again awoke. My head still thrummed with pain, but it was manageable. I blinked sleep away as I took in my surroundings, gained my bearings, and remembered where I was and the likely reason I was there. The sound of wood scraping against stone proceeded the soft, shuffled steps of a person entering my cell.

The light from the lantern Master Codiff held cast deep shadows over his hard face, making it look even more sinister than usual. I pulled myself up to a sitting position, straightening my back, preparing myself for whatever he had to say. He cast a wicked smile my way and moved toward the small stool, taking a seat with a flip of his robes before turning to stare at me.

We remained silent for long beats, neither willing to speak first, until Codiff asked, "How fare you, Roselle?"

The lack of title was a blatant omission meant to sting, but I had more pressing concerns at the moment. "Why am I locked in this tower?"

"For your protection and the protection of Ingar. We cannot have a dragon roaming the keep, can we?" He didn't wait for an answer before turning from me, seemingly unconcerned with it all. He pulled a small tinder from the sleeve of his robe and used it to light the candle with his lantern's fire. "There now. A little light." He laughed, a cruel chuckle. "Little Light. How apt for so many reasons." Turning back toward me with a sneer, he said, "I doubt we shall hear that name again in your lifetime."

My face was stone as I stared at him, but my heart twisted at the truth of his words. After some silence I asked, "Is my lifetime to be short?"

Codiff looked offended at the question. "Of course not, Roselle. We are not monsters to kill poor, lowly women."

"There's been plenty of women killed here, in many forms. Do not pretend otherwise." Anger rose in me, but I did not feel the corresponding heat I so often felt when anger took hold.

"True. Yet you are different. A lady by birth and marriage. Makes killing you more complicated, especially as you still have so much value."

"Oh, I know all about your planning and plotting with Lord Baxter. The real reason he, and you, pushed for a union between Blaine and me."

"Smart girl, though I doubt you know all." He rose then to crouch in front of me. "For instance," he said, before he snatched my arm in a punishing grip and traced a wrinkled finger from the wrist to the crease of my elbow.

I shuddered in disgust before trying, but failing, to twist away. We fought, his hold strong and bruising, before he lashed out with his words and knowledge.

"Dragons' blood holds magic, magic I can extract and use in a number of helpful and delightful ways. I kill you too soon, I lose access to all your fiery blood."

I finally managed to wrest my arm from his grip and surge to my feet, but it cost a shred of fabric. Once again, a vision from my dream came to life as Codiff smiled coldly at the scrap of frost-blue satin he rubbed between his fingers. He acted unfazed, unafraid, and I felt no power in me come to my defense. I had a flash of realization as I had in the Great Hall. Codiff somehow knew my magic was not functioning, and he would not place himself alone with me otherwise, as careful and cautious as the mage was. He knew, and had likely caused, my magic to not respond to my pull, my anger—my need.

Still, I was young and nimble, and it took nothing for me to kick out a foot and topple the crouched figure over on his backside. He jumped up, his face red with outrage at my nerve, and used his height to loom over my shorter form in an attempt to intimidate, dominate.

"It seems you still do not appreciate your position." He seethed, spittle flying into my face.

I did not flinch or back down. "It seems you have done something to make yourself feel brave. Much braver than you were in the Great Hall."

He smirked. "Aye. There are ways to ensure you are no real danger while reaping the benefits I and Ingar both require. I can use your blood regardless of your personal access to the magic." He paused to leer as he scraped a stare up and down my body. "Lord Ingar... Well, his needs are more physical and basic. No magic necessary for you to produce an heir."

I pulled straight, stepping away to give myself distance. I tried not to let it show, but his words caused fear to race down my spine. I folded my arms in silent defiance as he himself straightened and stepped away, a fighter sizing up his opponent before another round began.

"You are trapped here, in this tower, until I say you are free to leave."

"You say? Not Blaine?"

"Poor Lord Ingar has taken the discovery of your true nature quite hard, I'm afraid. He now relies solely on my counsel in these regards."

"Will he not see me?"

"I am unsure, although it is irrelevant. I will decide your fate here. If you behave, submit to my needs and the needs of Lord Ingar without fuss or disruption, I may see my way to freeing you. One day."

Turning his back toward me, he moved to fetch his lantern. Before drawing away from the table, he stooped to blow out the candle. Looking back at me, he said, "Can't leave you with fire, can we?"

Before he reached the door, he paused, his back still toward me. "I wonder how you feel about our power and positions in Ingar Keep now?" Without a backward glance, he slipped from the room, his steps swift and sure, so fast I hit the door as he locked the outside. I screamed in frustration, fear, and rage. It was the scream of any woman, not the roar of a dragon, yet it still burned my throat. As did my tears.

Twenty

I STARED OUT THE open window for hours, or at least what felt like hours. I knew nothing of telling time via the progress of the moon. Even if I did, there was no moon in sight, only soft reflections peeking behind a sweep of deep cloud cover. When my mind and body became too sluggish to hold myself up any longer, I curled on the mattress to find fitful yet dreamless sleep again.

I bolted upright when I heard shuffling outside the locked door. The scraping of metal on metal told me someone would enter, and I jumped to my feet, prepared to find Codiff's mocking face once again. When the door slowly swung open, Blaine stood there instead. His usual demeanor was off. He was tall and proud but also stepped with caution into the room. His presence felt somewhat hesitant, maybe even fearful. The look though. The look he gave me, one not of indulgence or lust but of cold assessment, as if I were danger about to strike, stabbed into my heart and ground into my gut with an icy sadness I knew I would feel for a long while.

"Woman," he said, a curt gruffness to his tone I was unused to hearing.

"Lord Ingar," I whispered back.

He looked around the room. Whether it was to assess the area and any possible dangers, to acquaint himself with my new home, or to avoid my gaze, I could not tell. After some silence, he looked back at me, and his perusal of my face snagged at my temple, the knot I could still feel slightly throbbing there. "Do you require assistance with your injury?"

It was such a cold, perfunctory question, one asked to any person, not a wife or a lover. Hearing it was like a blow to my middle. It robbed me of breath momentarily, and all I could do was blink at him in reply. Finally, with too much hurt in my tone for my liking, I croaked out, "Blaine."

I leaned forward, reaching for him, hoping he would prove my fears wrong and give me the chance to explain, but he stepped away swiftly, throwing a hand up between us as if to ward me off, protect himself from me.

"No further, Lady Ingar."

"Roselle. Your Little Light," I gritted out with a note of sarcasm on the pet name, my hurt now mixing with anger and outrage at this man who was supposed to care for me.

He ignored my words, pulling himself straight and clasping his hands firmly behind his back. Looking down from his height, his eyes were hard and unyielding. "I decided you will remain here, in this room. It is the safest option for Ingar and for you. We will assess in the future. For now, I will provide you with the bare minimum: food and shelter."

"That is all? No time? No talk?"

"I do not need to hear your lies," he said with clear anger in his tone. "The lies your kind spew."

"What of my truths? What of the fact Codiff and your father knew who and what I was? They maneuvered you to marry me because of what I am. Do you not care about such manipulations?"

"As I said, lies. Master Codiff was as shocked as the rest of us when you revealed your hidden self."

"You think what? That I lied about who I was, forced you into marriage to snare you in some trap?"

"Aye."

I exploded, rushing forward, the heat of anger starting to tingle in my body, until I was inches from his face. "How, exactly, did a nine-year-old orphan girl manipulate your father and a guardian into agreeing to a betrothal long before I came of age? Or do you conveniently forget facts in favor of the lies you've lived with your entire life?"

"Don't speak to me of lies, creature," he hissed, pushing back into my face, his anger replacing his fear. "I know not the levels of your machinations, the outlines of your plots. I need not know, as you have now exposed yourself."

"Exposed myself as what, exactly?"

"Dragon."

"Did you know dragons were people?" I pressed, needing this answer, finally not afraid to ask.

"Not people. No. Never people. Things. Vile things crawling this earth. Hidden for a time in human guise perhaps, but never actual people."

I shook with rage and hate, seeing Blaine for what he was, a man who would never question but always believe what he had believed as a young man, never understanding growth and change with the acquisition of new knowledge made people better, stronger, and more just and true. He would remain entrenched and saw no problems with this, remaining the Lord Ingar his father had created. I severed whatever ties binding us in my mind in the face of the truth he refused to see though he had the knowledge to see them properly. In the realization of his true acts of wanton brutality and murder. I stepped back, retreating not in fear but in order to reassess. My world was shattering around me, and for long silent breaths I knew not what to say or do.

Blaine breached the silence, barking orders. "You are still my wife. That cannot change until death. I still require a child, an heir—"

I cut him off, my voice like the crack of a whip when I hissed, "You will never touch me as a husband again."

"Do not think I wish it."

"Does not matter if you wish it or not. Touch me, and you will pay dearly."

He snorted, dismissing my threat. "You have no power here, dragon. In this room, in this keep, in all of Ingar. I am the power. The law. You will bow to my will."

"As you bow to the mage?" I sneered.

In a flash he was on me, pushing me back against the cold, hard stone walls and pinning me in with his height and weight, his hands slapping the stone at both sides of my head. It was odd, to feel the rage and tension between us in this pose, a position familiar but before tinged with care or lust. There was none between us now.

"I am Lord Blaine Ingar, and you live by my leave," he bit out. "You will do as I say, when I say, or else I will mount your head on the wall in my Great Hall."

I felt it then, the tingle of heat, faint but persistent under my skin. It was not enough to do anything, but enough to be a comfort and provide hope. I was about to clip back a rebuttal or maybe a growl in reply, I did not rightly know, but a soft tap on the oak door interrupted me. Blaine turned his head to look toward the entrance, and I saw beyond him at Lady Maria positioned between two guards as she balanced a tray in one hand.

She gave a deep curtsey, despite the tray, and kept her eyes averted as she said, "Lord Ingar, pardon my interruption."

He grunted and pushed off the wall, turning from me quickly to survey her. "Please set the food on the table and leave, Lady Maria."

His tone was soft, courteous, and respectful. Even kind. Everything it was not with me moments before so that every part of the short sentence stung. Neither seemed to note it as Lady Maria moved with grace to deposit my breakfast on the low table. She wobbled slightly, however, and tipped over the teacup on the tray, spilling tea on the floor. "Oh, no. I do apologize, my lord. So clumsy of me."

She crouched to wipe up the spill, pulling a dainty handkerchief from her sleeve to do so, but Blaine grabbed her gently by the arm and raised her up. She left the cloth lying there, stained with tea and whatever dirt had been stuck to the stone.

"No need for such, my lady. Please, be on your way."

Maria inclined her head in response and made a small hand gesture at me before pointedly looking back at her handkerchief. She did not bend to take it, only stared at it a moment before hanging her head and exiting the room.

Blaine sighed, rubbing his head as if it hurt, and looked back at me. "I will return in the evening. Perhaps you will be more civil then." Without even a glance behind, he stalked from the room, then slammed and locked the door as I looked after the man who was my husband but seemed like a stranger.

I shook my head on a sigh. It did little good to dwell on the idea of a loving husband and partner in life, something recent events had irrevocably revealed I never had. I did, however, wait a long minute before rushing to the handkerchief in case Blaine decided to return for some reason. Lady Maria had been subtle but clear. There was something for me in the piece of cloth.

The beautifully embroidered handkerchief displayed with the intricate floral pattern she favored in her work. There were extra stitches in the corner, stitches creating a tiny, protective fold of fabric. I removed them as gently as possible, patiently loosening the thread and unsewing each stitch. When I freed the thread, I unfolded the corner to find a tiny slip of paper with a brief message on it. "Codiff doses your drinks."

I looked at the tea, spilled and undrinkable on the floor, then at the tin cup of water left on the tray. It was cool, I could tell, as a tiny sheen of droplets formed around the outside of the cup. My mouth was dry, in desperate need of refreshment. Yet I trusted Lady Maria. She risked much to give me such information. I would not disregard it. The toast and dried meat on the tray looked unappetizing given my thirst, but a small cucumber also rested there, oddly out of place given the theme of the other food. I smiled then, for what felt like the first time in ages, thinking about Lady Maria placing the crisp, refreshing bit of food there.

I sat at the table, pushing everything away save the cucumber, which I bit into with a loud snap. As I ate, I considered what I knew, and

I stoked the power I felt growing again inside. More than anything, I hoped for answers in the dreams to come.

TWENTY-ONE

THE SUNLIGHT WANED AND the sky turned from orange to pink to navy blue before Blaine returned to my cell. I had thrown my water out the window long before but left the dried food on the tray in overt protest. Blaine shook his head and called in a guard to switch out trays. My evening meal was the same except there was no cucumber to be had, only tea, water, dry toast, and jerky. I turned my nose up at the meal and Blaine growled, saying he would force feed me if required. He needed me alive to bear children after all.

Codiff lurked in the doorframe, surveying my food, my empty cups from the previous meal, and the exchange with Blaine. His bland smile was enough to transmit Lady Maria had been correct. He had no fear of me because he thought my magic suppressed, by whatever concoction he poured into the water and tea. Both men gave remarks, made declarations about what they expected me do and be, how my life would unfold from that point forward. I stared and said nothing, standing tall and proud and firm in my resolve. They promised more discussions and made a few more demands, and I let them. It mattered not if my power grew and held. I knew I would free myself soon enough, even if I was unsure how or when.

I poured the tea and water down the outside wall from the window ledge, sad to see it go, as thirst still clung to me. I wondered how long it would be before dehydration overtook my resolve. The toast appeared dry and therefore safe, so I ate it, needing something to fill my stomach, though it felt and tasted like ash in my mouth. I swallowed hard, keeping it down somehow. During this, and for the long day that followed, I sat thinking, breathing, feeling for the strengthening fire rumbling in my blood. When I tired, I lay down to sleep and hoped for a dream.

In the past, whenever dreaming, I acted if something occurred or I observed the dream from afar. Thinking the day away, I knew my dreams could help me end my captivity, give me knowledge I desperately needed, but I did not have time to waste. I determined I must be proactive in my dream, direct my actions and take control of what happened rather than simply reacting. When the hazy smoke appeared in my mind, I did not slowly lift through it. I swam instead of listlessly floating and reached a solid footing quickly. I ran headfirst into the vision of my mother on the mountainside of Ingar. She smiled softly, and I tried my tongue. It was thick and sticky, unused to being present in my dreams. I managed a single question after much strain: "What do I do?"

My mother frowned, took my hand, and looked out at the clouds. "You follow the fire down. You will crack open, but oh, my love, you will also soar." She pulled me close for a hug so fierce it rattled my bones, so deep and soothing I felt it in my soul, before she pulled back. "Go," she whispered, and laid a soft finger on my forehead.

My eyes opened to the cell, the straw mattress, the hammering in my heart, and a plan forming in my mind.

I sat up the remainder of the night, pulling on the thread of my fire. Dawn came and went, hesitant guards brought me food, but I remained still, testing my fire and doing what my mother had bidden in my dreams. Around midday, the sun bright and blazing in the middle of the sky, something in me tugged back, an anchor on the magic I spun into spool in my head. I tugged harder, pulled myself down in the dark of my mind, the thin orange flame guiding my way, until I hit a hard block of ice. Except it was not ice, but heated crystal the color of my eyes, the color of my now soiled dress, a blue so vivid it glowed. I looked on this thing, buried in my mind, with awe and reverence. Felt the pulse of its contained power. My hands skimmed the rough surface, and I felt a soft heat penetrate my skin. I gently pressed against the thing with my index finger and felt a hollow resonance within. Some sense told me I needed to get inside the outer crust, break it apart to reach the hollow within the glowing shield.

I pounded with my fists. Tugged the cord of flame spooled at my side. I kicked and scratched, trying to break it open. I used all the strength I could manifest in my mind. Pulled on all I had in me and shoved it toward the crystal: my magic, my desire, my will, my knowledge, and me as a whole. A small crack appeared and I jumped on it, prying my fingers in to widen and pull and feeling it tear as if I were tearing my own flesh apart. Flames leaped free, singeing my hands and burning them to ash. I watched it fade and drift away on a wind, a scream pouring from my throat until the fire licked there too, diving deep into my body to burn me from the inside out.

Oh, did I burn. A pain I could never describe scattered across my flesh, my bones cracking and searing. I opened my eyes, hoping for relief from my mental pain, but saw it echoed in the real world. My limbs charred, growing instead of shrinking, twisting and turning and pulling into something wholly new but not entirely different than what I had been before.

Light and color intensified as my vision shifted. My smell and sound heightened so much, I noted every individual in the bailey below and what they had eaten for midday meal. My body became tall and strong but lean, twice my normal size. The ash and embers fell from where my flesh had been, and I saw iridescent skin underneath, scales over powerful muscles flowing into talons. My tongue licked out and lashed at my teeth, wicked sharp and large in my mouth. My back muscles pulled and stretched until they split apart along an invisible seam. Wings unfurled as if, unknown to me, they had always itched there beneath the skin.

I had no mirror, no way of fully seeing my transformation. It did not matter. My body lifted off the ground as I flapped my wings. I could fly, at least partially. I hoped it was enough to get me clear of the keep, off Ingar land, as far from this place as possible. Except, the easiest exit was no longer accessible given my new size, my leathery wingspan taking up much of the space in the now cramped cell.

Fire rumbled in my gut, churning, pushing me forward despite the lack of clear exit. I trusted myself now, in what I felt and knew even if it all existed in some new body, and let it out with a deafening roar. The answering blaze shot toward the window, singeing the stone, doing little until it glowed blue, then white with heat and began to melt. I had little time. I could hear screams below and the rattle of incoming armor from the tower steps. I grabbed the melting stone with my talons, unfazed by the heat, and ripped it away, enough so I could step fully out in the sunshine from the hole torn in the side of the tower.

I looked out at the clear blue sky, did not look back at the shouts from behind me, the commands I could hear given in Blaine's voice, or the screams of rage and disappointment from Codiff. I crouched and jumped, spreading my wings wide, catching the air and lifting myself higher and higher with quick, powerful beats of my new wings. I headed closer to the mountains, moving faster than I ever imagined. Strong and unstoppable. Something old and new.

I circled the edges of Ingar Keep at a distance, out of range of any arrows or spears yet close enough to see the place and people. The view was like my tapestry, except Blaine swore and seethed at the melted edges of the tower, surrounded by guards, with Codiff red-faced at his side. The dragon-eye view of Ingar, my short-lived and little-known home, made me recall the people who had helped me: Palle, Andra, Milly, and Lady Maria. I could not help them if I left them behind. I shook off the thought. Strategic retreat was necessary, did not signal defeat. Even if Blain did not like the idea, I was by law and right still Lady Ingar, and in my new form, with more knowledge of my power and magic, I may one day be able to bring about change. Yet, that was time away, a future I could not reach, much less predict, if I did not escape on my swift wings while I had the means to do so.

Soaring beyond, out of range and hearing and experience, I turned my new face toward the sun to drive away my darker thoughts and misgivings, to bask in the freedom of the sky and bright light. I felt a tug on the thread of my fire, a pull toward something else. Something west. Some instinct long dormant told me it was a place, a haven far from Ingar, far from any I knew. Possibly a new home where the dreams of dragons came to life.

ACKNOWLEDGMENTS

There are many great things about being an author. One of my favorites is getting to thank people in writing. First, I have to thank Ario, my husband, for being so very supportive of this author dream I have. Second, I have to thank all the people who made this book a thing. Nicole Wells made the amazing cover and it is simply lovely. The cover was done before the book was, so it definitely helped my writing process. Janna and Angie at Novel Nurses Editing Services were amazing. Sharp, thoughtful editors and proofreaders for my work. Thanks for all you did to make my words more polished. A big shout out to my new ARC Team for taking the time to read early and give me feedback. It was so beneficial. Finally, thanks to all my friends and family, for always being their and stepping up with the support.

ABOUT THE AUTHOR

Sonya Lawson is a recovering academic currently writing fantasy, light and dark, in a variety of subgenres. Some might say she switches it up too much, but her stories have at least one common characteristic — sassy, intelligent women trying to do the best they can in whatever world they inhabit.

While she remains a rural Kentuckian at heart, she currently lives in the Pacific Northwest where she fills her days with writing, editing, reading, walking old forests, and watching sitcoms or horror films. You can find more information about current projects and upcoming releases at www.sonyalawson.com.

Want to read more by Sonya? You can find information about all her other books at https ://sonyalawson.com/books.

Want to hear more about all her projects and get freebies first? Join her newsletter at https://www.subscribepage.com/k9v0u9.

You can also follow her on all her socials in order to stay connected. Find her on TikTok, Instagram, and Facebook under her username @sonyalawsonwrites.

Or, find all this info and so much more on her linktree - https://linktr.ee/sonyalawsonwrites.